Koos Verkaik

ISBN: 978-93-91103-44-6
eISBN: 978-81-96109-32-5

©Publisher

Publisher: Pharos Books (P) Ltd.
Plot No.-55, Main Mother Dairy Road
Pandav Nagar, East Delhi-110092
Phone: 011-40395855, +4049916623
WhatsApp: +91 8368220032
E-mail: sales@pharosbooks.in
Website: www.pharosbooks.in
First Edition: 2023

Children's Short Stories
By Koos Verkaik

Short stories for children; adventures in the hot summer and the cold winter… Stories of all seasons and about a variety of themes, that will make everyone smile.

Animals and elves, snowmen and knights, sultans and kings, smart girls and clever boys – they all turn up in an avalanche of exciting tales!

'Pancakes for the prince…', 'The shivering little polar bear…', 'The nicest snakes in the forest…', 'The dancing kangaroo…', 'Ice cubes for the sultan…' and many, many more stories that will give you a good feeling; enjoy them all!

Koos Verkaik is a master storyteller, who has written more than 70 different novels and series of children's books.

He wrote the extensive, famous series Alex and the Wolpertinger and the beautiful series Saladin the Wonder Horse.

This exciting collection of children's stories has been published before in different magazines.

CONTENTS

1. THE ICE PARTY 7
2. PANCAKES FOR THE PRINCE 10
3. THE DORMOUSE IS A LIE-ABED… OR NOT? 15
4. THE SILENT MOLE 18
5. A SMART MONKEY 21
6. HOW LITTLE BEAVER GOT HIS NAME 24
7. THE SHIVERING LITTLE POLAR BEAR 27
8. THE SWALLOW AND THE SPARROW 31
9. TALL STORIES FROM AN OLD PENGUIN 34
10. LITTLE JASPER, THE WOODCUTTER'S SON 37
11. THE BIG BEAVER BROOK IN THE FOREST 45
12. THE LITTLE KNIGHT 51
13. CONJURER OR WIZARD 56
14. THE ADVENTURE OF THE CROW 59
15. THE NICEST SNAKES IN THE FOREST 62
16. THE SQUIRREL AND THE WOODPECKER 67
17. THE DANCING KANGAROO 71
18. THE GOLDEN MAGIC LIZARD 74
19. FLIGHT TO CHINA 78
20. THE MUSICAL CAT 82
21. WHAT KIND OF DOG IS THIS? 86
22. THE EXHAUSTED ZOOKEEPER 90
23. CAT AND MOUSE 94
24. A COAT FOR JACK FROST 97
25. A FINCH ON HOLIDAY 100
26. UMBRELLA ISLAND 103
27. ICE CUBES FOR THE SULTAN 106
28. THE PRINCESS AND THE ELVES 109
29. THE CHICKENS AND THE RABBIT 112
30. THE BIGGEST LIE 116
31. CASPER AND HIS DOG 120
32. A POOL FULL OF ANIMALS 124
33. FROZEN ELVES 128
34. A GOOD IDEA FROM A LITTLE SQUIRREL 131
35. THE BIGGEST SNOWMAN 134

THE ICE PARTY

Blackbush, a little village, lay somewhere by a river. And Crownwood, another village, was across the river.

There was no bridge on the river. One could only go from Blackbush to Crownwood, or from Crownwood to Blackbush if one had the possession of a boat or money for the ferry.

But in winters, when a solid floor of ice covered the river, people could walk from one village to another and that was something they celebrated; then, they loved to hold an Ice Party!

Friends and families visited each other and everyone loved to skate on the ice.

Everyone had a good time and there was a fair on both sides of the river.

Those were the most beautiful days of the year for the Blackbushers and the Crownwooders.

But there had not been a sharp frost for many years. Every now and then, there was a keen frost for one night only and that was by far not enough to form a solid sheet of ice. There were many children in both villages now, who had never experienced the great Ice Party in their lives. Again and again one hoped for a hard winter. But it did not happen.

Rianne was a little girl who dreamt of walking to the other side on ice someday. She lived in Blackbush herself. Her cousin lived beyond, in Crownwood.

One day she wrote a little letter to King Winter:

Dear King Winter,

Will you please bring us a hard winter? I want to go to the Ice Party

and I want to skate to the other side of the river to visit my niece Anna

in Crownwood.

Thank you very much in advance.

Greetings from Rianne.

She put the letter in an old wooden shoe which she put into the water. The current took the wooden shoe along and soon it had vanished from sight behind a bend in the river.

Winter set in, but it felt more like autumn. There was a storm, there was rain, but there was no frost at all.

One day the postman brought a letter for Rianne. She opened it. It contained a short message.

She read:

"Hello, Rianne! Your wish will come true. Pretty soon there will be a sharp frost and then you can go to Crownwood to see your cousin. I will personally see to that! With kindest regards, King Winter."

Of course, she was delighted and she showed the message to everyone. Her parents did not believe a thing about it:

"Someone has found your little letter and plays a joke on you now."

Everyone in Blackbush thought the same way.

But… two days later winter set in. After three days there was ice on the river. It took only one week to make the ice strong enough to be able to skate on it. And after ten days the ice was thick enough for the Ice Party!

For the first time in many years, the people from both villages met again. Rianne skated together with her cousin Anna. Everyone came to talk to Rianne. Although no one believed a single word of the message, one agreed that it was very special that winter had set in after the postman had brought that mysterious letter.

There was a fair in both villages. The Ice Party lasted till late at night and then colourful lanterns burned everywhere. The fairground showmen had come from far. The owner of the merry-go-round, that stood on the dyke in Blackbush, shook his head in disbelief and spoke in a loud voice:

"It is so cold here! Oh, one could easily freeze up here!"

"Of course!" said a Blackbusher. "It is winter! Finally! Winter! Everywhere!"

"Well, that is not exactly true," said the man of the merry-go-round. "Ten miles further on, upstream, there is no ice in the river. Ten miles the other way, downstream, there is no ice on the river as well. I can only conclude that King Winter decided this year to produce sharp frost in Blackbush and Crownwood only!"

The news passed from mouth to mouth. And then, yes… then everyone knew for sure.

The Ice Party was due to the letter of Rianne – the letter that had driven away in a wooden shoe down the river and that, somewhere on its way, was found by none other than King Winter.

2

PANCAKES FOR THE PRINCE

Prince Squeak gazed sadly outside through the kitchen window. He had seldom felt so bored before. Because his father was the king, he got the most beautiful toys in the land and because his father wanted the best of everything, the most clever cook was in lead in the kitchen of the palace.

Prince Squeak loved pancakes, he wanted them every day. He preferred to eat them with butter and icing sugar. And preferably with so much icing sugar that it made the pancake invisible and he had to search for it with his fork.

But today he could not bear the sight of pancakes anymore!

He had not played with his toys today. Not with his big bear, not with the shining crown of the king and not with his new kite. And when the cook had brought him a pile of hot pancakes, he had said immediately:

"Bah! I am not in the mood for them at all. And that is because you are the worst cook in the land. You should better go home right away, for we cannot use cooks like you in our stately palace."

The cook left. But before leaving he had gone to the king to tell him what had happened.

The king pondered on it. He pondered for a long, long time. And then, all of a sudden, he knew what to do. He called his ministers together and said to them:

"Get on your horses and go out in the country, right away. Search for the best cooks around. For my son is hungry for pancakes and our own cook obviously has no idea how to make them."

The truth was, that the cook had done his very best and had covered the pancakes with lots of icing sugar as asked. He didn't understand what was happening; who could make tastier pancakes than him?

In the meantime all Prince Squeak did was stare sadly out of the kitchen window. Every now and then he rubbed his belly and then he shook his head. Just imagine, such a pert cook to serve him odd pancakes like that!

Through the window, he saw the gates of the palace open. And then Prince Squeak suddenly felt a lot merrier. What did he see? The ministers returned. And they were not alone…

A small army of cooks turned up behind them. It was such an amusing sight. There were thick cooks and thin cooks, cooks wearing a high, white chef's hat and cooks wearing a long apron.

The door of the kitchen swung open and all the cooks stepped inside. They said together:

"Prince Squeak, we will make you some nice pancakes! You just wait and see!"

They bowed for the little prince and then they set to work. The big kitchen was full of pans. Prince Squeak watched how the mixture was made and how the cooks poured it into the pans – it all happened in a short time. Soon the cooks stood in line, all holding a big white plate in their hands with a hot pancake covered with icing sugar.

"You should taste this one," suggested one of the cooks.

"No, no, taste my pancake! For this one is the tastiest," said another one.

And Prince Squeak tasted all of them. Till his stomach was so full that it was impossible for him to take another bite. But not a single pancake had been to his liking. They all tasted just as strange as the one the cook of the palace had served him.

"Go home. All of you," he said disillusioned. "I have an appetite for nothing anymore, not even for pancakes because you are not able to make them properly."

Of course, the king was at his wits' end when he heard about this. How could he reign peacefully when his subjects weren't even able to make tasty pancakes for his son? He sat down on his thrown and stroked his beard despondently.

Then there was a knock on the door.

"Come in…" muttered the king.

The door opened and the little alley boy stepped inside.

"Sire," he said, "I am very sorry to disturb you, but will you please allow me to tell you something? It is about Prince Squeak."

The King let the boy talk and understood everything that was going on.

"You are so right," he said, after the little alley boy had finished his story. "Now you just go ahead…"

The little alley boy pranced out of the room and went to the kitchen. Prince Squeak still sat there grumbling.

"I will make you the best pancakes you ever tasted, Prince Squeak," said the little alley boy.

Prince Squeak shrugged his shoulders.

The little alley boy set to work. First, he went to get wood for the cooker. He didn't seem to be in a hurry. Then he went searching for the right pan and the ingredients and strangely enough that took him almost an hour. And it took him one more hour to get the mixture ready.

Prince Squeak said:

"Why don't you work a little faster? I'm beginning to get hungry."

But the little alley boy did not even seem to hear him and it took again one hour at least before he put a pan on the fire. And then, finally, he started to bake his first pancake. Only one. And that particular pancake smelled very, very good…

"Oh, I think I will like that!" said Prince Squeak. "Give it to me right now, oh, that pancake smells so good, it must be delicious."

The little alley boy ate the pancake himself instead and only after a long time did he start to bake a second one. He gave it to the prince, whose mouth was watering…

The prince devoured it.

"Oh, yes," he said. "You are right. This is the best pancake I ever ate!"

"Thank you, sire. " said the little alley boy. "But I must tell you something. It was our own cook who taught me how to bake a pancake like that. The reason why you didn't like his pancakes was that you had already eaten so much all day long. Nothing will taste good anymore after gobbling the whole day because your stomach is full. Doesn't that sound logical to you?"

Prince Squeak thought it over. After some time he nodded yes.

"I guess you're right," he said. "Better ask our cook to come back. I promise that I won't gobble so much anymore."

The king stood by the door and had heard everything. He said to the little alley boy:

"I know what you should do now. Use the mixture to make pancakes for me and for yourself."

He sat down at the kitchen table and the little alley boy was very pleased to be invited to eat together with the king.

Prince Squeak was staring out the window again. But this time he was smiling.

"Tomorrow," he thought, "tomorrow I will have an ordinary slice of bread and cheese… And I promise that I will even eat the crusts…"

3

THE DORMOUSE IS A LIE-ABED... OR NOT?

Have you ever heard of a dormouse? Ordinary mice are very busy creatures, always looking for food and never seeming to have time for any rest. But a dormouse might as well be named a lie-abed. That is because this rodent has no problem sleeping for about… seven months! So a dormouse is not so adventurous at all. He spends most of his life in his cosy home.

But Rebel Dormouse was a strong, young mouse and didn't feel like snoring for such a long, long time at all.

"Oh no, not for me!" he told everyone he came across. "I prefer to stay awake!"

"A dormouse must eat lots of food and get fat," someone explained to him. "When it gets colder, he can creep into a hollow tree or a hole and won't get hungry when he is fast asleep. A year has twelve months. Dormice stuff themselves for five months and then they will sleep for seven months at a stretch. That's the way it has always been and that's the way it will always be."

"You do as you please," said Rebel Dormouse. "All that sleeping… isn't that just a waste of time?"

He became friends with a group of wood mice who were wide awake all the time and who laughed, played and jumped around. He really had a good time with them. They crossed the fields together, in search of food. When it began to get colder, the wood mice found a nice place under the wooden floor of a house that stood in the middle of a forest. There they built up their food supplies and fitted up their nests.

"I feel at home here," said Rebel. "It is so comfortable and warm."

He laid himself down on a bed of dried grass and realized he was a happy rodent. The wood mice talked to each other. Listening to their familiar voices, Rebel Dormouse closed his eyes…

"Rebel! Rebel! Wake up!" he heard suddenly.

Slowly he opened his eyes. He was still lying there on his bed of grass. When he sat up straight and looked down, he was startled out of his wits! Where had his fat belly gone? He was as thin as a rake and all of a sudden he was getting very hungry. The wood mice were standing round him and stared at him with a worried glance in their big black eyes.

"Would you like something to eat?" asked a wood mouse.

"Yes, please… And I am so thirsty…"

Rebel ate and drank. Finally, he was wide awake and he said:

"Well, friends, I think I have slept for a little while. But now I feel completely rested and I am ready for new adventures."

The wood mice burst out laughing. Rebel had no idea what was going on.

"What's the matter with you?" he asked. "Are you making fun of me?"

"No, no, of course not," said someone. "It just sounded so funny when you mentioned that you had slept for a while. You have been snoring for seven months!"

"Really?" asked Rebel in surprise. "How can that be?"

"Very simple," was the answer. "A dormouse sleeps for seven months on end. There is nothing they can do about that, for that is what dormice do. And it is no use acting as tough as you do, Rebel, for you are a dormouse yourself and when you sleep… you sleep for seven months."

"I understand," muttered Rebel. "Now I know what I am… a real dormouse, a real lie-abed…"

"But you are also our friend," said the wood mouse. "You must never forget about that. We differ from you, you differ from us. We like to stay awake as long as possible, you like to sleep as long as you can. No problem, Rebel… you are the best friend of all wood mice!"

"I feel so happy…" said Rebel. And then he continued with a smile:

"Is there something to eat, friends? I am getting hungry again…"

The wood mice had a good laugh, they tapped him on the back and brought him the most delicious fruits and seeds.

They were glad that their friend was awake again… for… five months!

4

THE SILENT MOLE

At the edge of the forest was an open spot between the high grass. Every night little animals from the forest and the field gathered there to talk to each other. They always had a great time there. There the hedgehog could meet with the toad, the lizard and the frog had time to chat and the mouse and the beetle told about their adventures.

Sometimes the ground began to move and then a mole popped up. He blinked his eyes against the light of the setting sun and sat down on top of his molehill in silence.

"That is Moly the mole," a big dragonfly said. "He does not see much with these little eyes of him, but he can hear us very well. I think he likes to be with us every now and then to listen to us. For the rest, he prefers to be on his own."

The mole never spoke a word. With a smile on his snout, he sat there listening in silence and after some time he disappeared under the ground again.

"Till the next time, Moly the mole!" shouted the animals. "And remember, you are always welcome here!"

Not so long ago, on a hot summer day, something terrible happened. The forest was on fire! Fire and flames came from all directions. And so the animals were trapped! They gathered on the open spot coughing from the smoke and fearing the upcoming fire. They were in a panic!

"What are we supposed to do?" wailed the hedgehog. "We are trapped, we are surrounded by the fire!"

"Even I cannot go through it, no matter how high I jump!" said the squirrel.

"I'm starting to dry up," moaned a frog.

Only the beetle could escape because he could spread his wings and fly away.

"But I will stay with you for as long as I can," he sighed.

All of a sudden the ground moved. The mole popped up.

"Moly! Stay away from here!" cried the animals. "The forest is on fire! The entire field is ablaze! This is the most terrible place to be!"

Then, for the very first time, they heard the voice of the mole.

"Friends, I am here to help you. For you have always been so nice to me and I have always loved listening to your stories. No one can dig as well as I and my tunnels lead deep under the ground to an old foxhole. It is shut off from the outside world, but I am able to reach it. There it is safe for all animals. Follow me, come creeping behind me as quick as you can and pull all the loose ground outside. Quick, quick! It is too smoky here and soon the fire will reach all of you!"

He turned around and started to dig.

The hedgehog followed him and kicked the soil away with his hind paws. All the other animals followed and together they widened the tunnels that the mole dug. Above their heads was a sea of flames now… But they reached the foxhole safely and sat there together in the darkness.

"Thank you so much, Moly," said the animals. "You have rescued us."

"No trouble at all," thought the mole. "This is what friends are for!"

One day later the animals ventured to leave the foxhole. The fire had destroyed everything and they moved to another place where they found trees and grass.

The first time they gathered there on an open spot on the edge of the forest, the ground began to move… Moly the mole popped up…

And again he opened his mouth to say something, although it was not much:

"I began to miss you…"

From that time on the mole always pops up when the animals gather at the open spot in the evening. He doesn't speak a word, all he does is listen. And there is always a smile on his snout, because he loves to sit there on top of his molehill and listen to what the others have to say…

5

A SMART MONKEY

Every time the director of the big circus announced Coco the monkey, the audience reacted with enthusiastic applause. Everyone sat on the edge of their chair and waited impatiently for the monkey to turn up. Coco entered the ring, dressed in a red jacket and red trousers. A group of screaming monkeys dressed in a blue jacket and blue trousers came after him. And they, in their turn, were followed by a beautiful horse.

Then the show would begin. Everyone knew already what was going to happen.

Coco the monkey would vanish into thin air! It was a great mystery how he managed to do so.

The orchestra started to play and the monkeys dressed in blue formed a circle around the horse. They danced around wildly and in the meantime, Coco jumped on the horse's back. There he stood, keeping himself in balance with stretched arms.

Not much later two clowns turned up. They stood in front of Coco, the horse and the dancing monkeys and held up a curtain with two long sticks.

For about two minutes the monkeys and the horse remained invisible behind the curtain.

The clowns let the curtains fall and from the audience came the sound of deep sighs and cries of astonishment.

There were the monkeys dressed in blue, dancing… there was the big, beautiful horse…

But Coco had disappeared, Coco had vanished into thin air!

The horse turned round and round. Coco remained invisible. There was no hole in the floor of the ring where Coco could slip through. There was no rope to make it possible for him to climb up.

For the second time, the clowns held up the curtain. When they let it fall again and the music suddenly stopped, the audience could see Coco standing on the back of the horse again!

There he was, in his nice, red clothes. He clapped his hands and looked proudly at the people. The monkey had done it again. He received thundering applause.

Now, Coco has become too old for circus acts and he is living in a big park now, where he leads a comfortable life. Now everyone is allowed to know how he managed to vanish into thin air.

Coco entered the ring dressed in red, followed by the other monkeys. He climbed on the back of the horse. The clowns held the curtain up. Immediately Coco took off his clothes… turned them inside out and put them on again. The jacket and the trousers were red on the outside and blue on the inside. Exactly as blue as the clothes from the dancing monkeys!

And no one was able to count the up-and-down jumping monkeys. Coco let himself fall down from the horse's back and started to dance along with the others.

The curtain fell and Coco had vanished into thin air: no one understood that he had become one of the many dancers now. Then things went on in reverse order. The curtain was put up. Coco jumped on the horse, turned his clothes inside out again and stood there in a red jacket and red trousers when the curtain came down again.

The smart monkey had learnt all this from the animal trainer of the circus. The animal trainer often visits the monkey in the big park. Then he strokes the back of the old Coco and says:

"You are the smartest monkey, Coco. You are the best!"

Then Coco nods yes two or three times and looks at him with his dark eyes as if he wants to say:

"I know, I know… And oh, I had such a great time when I performed my show in the circus!"

The animal trainer gives him a juicy apple and stays with him for a long time. For they are the very best friends…

6

HOW LITTLE BEAVER GOT HIS NAME

The Indian tribe lived for more than a hundred years on the bank of a wild streaming river. They always caught fish in the river, but no one ever dared to take a swim. That was too dangerous.

On a hot summer day, a little boy sat down on a stone near the river. He wiped the sweat from his forehead and then he heaved a deep sigh.

"Phew! It is so hot!"

How he would have loved to take a dive. But that was strictly forbidden. The water would drag him away! Therefore he remained sitting there and dreamt of a swim in the cool water.

All of a sudden he saw a little animal in the river, that struggled to keep its head above the water in a wild whirlpool. The boy swung into action right away. He found a long branch and reached out with it as far as possible over the river. The little animal reached out for it and clung to it with its paws. Now the boy had to use all his strength to draw the branch in, and he succeeded! The little animal was able to crawl onto the bank. It was only then that the boy saw what it actually was – a little beaver! Softly he stroked the animal's head and back.

"You better go back to your father and mother now and prevent yourself from landing in a whirlpool for the second time," said the little Indian.

The beaver ran away and dove into the river in a place where it was safe.

"If only I could swim in the river too, beaver!" said the little Indian in a loud voice.

The next morning the boy woke up early in his tent. His feet felt so strange and cold… He sat upright and gave a cry.

"There's water in my tent! How can that be? Water in the tent!"

Not much later all Indians were standing outside. The land on which they had set up their tents was flooded; the water reached up to their ankles! The wise chief understood what had happened.

"Beavers!" he said. "They like to build a big, solid dam in a river. That way a lake comes into being wherein they can live and build their homes. We will have to displace the tents, we must set them up a bit further inland. Now we don't live at the bank of the wild river any longer, but at the shore of a quiet lake…"

The chief went up to the little boy and asked:

"Didn't you rescue a beaver yesterday?"

The boy nodded yes.

"Well done," spoke the chief. "The beavers feel safe here. Thanks to you they understand that we are their friends. From now on we will call you Little Beaver."

The boy was proud of his name. And… two days later he was allowed to take a swim in the new lake, together with all his friends.

One day while swimming in the lake, he suddenly saw the little beaver again, whom he had saved. The boy and the beaver swam toward each other. They bumped their noses together and looked deeply into each other's eyes.

"Thanks," the boy laughed. "Finally we can get into the water. Beavers are wonderful animals. Do you know my name? Little Beaver! Isn't that beautiful?"

The beaver hit the water hard with its flat tail. Little Beaver slapped the water with the flat of his hand. From then on, that was their way of greeting each other...

The boy and the beaver have always remained the best of friends!

7

THE SHIVERING LITTLE POLAR BEAR

Mother Polar Bear stepped slowly through the snow. After her, came her three cubs: Bully, Woolly and Shiver. Bully was the largest one of the three cubs. He was also the most curious and brave little bear and had small, glittering, twinkling eyes. Woolly was like a fluffy tangle of white wool. Little Shiver came behind. He was the smallest of the three polar bears. And he didn't like the cold snow and the slippery Arctic ice. When you listened closely, you could hear his teeth clattering with the cold.

"Hurry up, little Shiver!" said mother bear. "You have to keep on walking, or else we'll never get to the water."

"We're going to catch fish," said Bully. "And that sounds very nice to me!"

"Yes, that's very nice indeed," said Woolly.

"And cold," said little Shiver.

Bully and Woolly climbed a high iceberg and slid down on their backs. With their paws in the air. They slipped past their mom. As soon as they got to the water, Mother Polar Bear told them to be very careful.

"You have to learn to swim before you can just play here," she said. "But first we're going to make sure we get something to eat, because I'm starving!"

She bent over the water and lashed out with a paw – a big fish landed on the ice. Bully and Woolly ran to it and within seconds there was nothing left of the fish. The second fish was for little Shiver. He thought his meal was cold, but because he was so hungry, he ate everything.

"Brr…" he sighed.

"You are such a chilly body," said Bully.

"You're a funny bear," Woolly teased. "You'd better live in a warm country."

Little Shiver didn't say anything. He was used to the teasing of his brothers and he also knew that they were somewhat right.

A polar bear is never cold, right?

Mother Polar Bear caught a few more fish and it wasn't long before everyone had eaten their fill.

Little Shiver thought:

"I don't want to be cold, I want to be a normal polar bear and play in the snow like my brothers."

Mother bear just lay down in the middle of the ice and soon fell asleep. She always went to sleep after she had eaten a lot.

"Shall we dig in the snow?" suggested Bully.

"Yes Nice!" said Woolly and he started immediately.

"Brrr!" Little Shiver said again and his brothers looked at him as if to say: "Have you ever seen such a strange polar bear...?"

Little Shiver sat down despondently in the snow. He looked around and all there was to see were snow-covered mountains, ice and water.

"Blub!" they heard.

A large, fat walrus had surfaced in the water. With such a huge moustache and a double chin. It seemed a very neat and distinguished animal, but when he saw the three bears on the edge of the ice, he boldly stuck out his tongue.

"What little ones you are," he said in a deep voice, "I don't think you can even swim yet. Well, then you should see me!"

The fat walrus went into hiding and slapped the water hard with its tail, sending the drops splashing all around. When he came up again, he said:

"You see? This is big fun..."

Bully became very angry. He ran to the water's edge and shouted:

"Did you really think we couldn't swim? Just wait..."

Woolly wanted to stop his brother, but Bully already splashed into the water. The fat walrus laughed so hard it shook his double chin. Because no matter what Bully tried, he almost couldn't keep himself afloat.

"Help!" he cried.

And Woolly also cried: "Oh, help! Help!"

But Mother Bear slept so soundly that she didn't hear. And the walrus watched and just kept laughing.

Now Little Shiver got angry. He got very angry! Why didn't that weird walrus help? He made a decision. Without a moment's hesitation, he also jumped into the cold water. His fur got all wet, but he didn't pay attention.

"I can swim," he thought to himself, "yes, I can swim!"

Little Shiver grabbed Bully by the neck and swam to the side again.

Fortunately Mother Bear had now woken up and she helped to bring the two brothers back to dry land.

"Go away quickly, chubby walrus!" she said. "Otherwise I'll teach you a lesson!"

The walrus went into hiding and was never seen again.

Little Shiver got a big kiss from his mother.

"You have been so brave, Little Shiver. You behaved like a real polar bear!"

Little Shiver looked at his mother and said:

"The water was so cold… It's much warmer here. Look at me… I don't even shiver anymore."

He shook out his white woolly fur, just like Bully.

"I'm not cold anymore!" then Little Shiver cheered. "Awesome! Brothers, shall we play in the snow?"

"You're a nice playmate," said Bully.

"And you are a real polar bear, just like us," said Woolly.

Soon the three of them were rolling through the snow.

Little Shiver loved it and from that day on he was never cold again…

THE SWALLOW AND THE SPARROW

Menno Sparrow and Pintail the Swallow knew each other from the time when they were both still babies and not yet able to fly. Menno lived under the roof tiles of a barn.

Pintail lived just below; there his parents had built a nest against the wall, just below the gutter. The little ones got along well. At first, they chattered to each other from their own nests. Then they met on the edge of the gutter.

There they held on tightly with their paws and flapped their wings. Pintail was the first to dare to let go of the edge and suddenly he flew in a wide circle around the barn and the farm.

"Try it too, Menno!" he cried. "It's so much fun to be able to fly!"

Menno tried and moments later he fluttered after Pintail! He would never learn to fly as fast as his friend, because what bird can overtake a swallow? They had a wonderful summer together. They flew over the fields, the forests, the rivers, the lakes, visited the villages and once even went to the big city. It was great to be such good friends. The swallow and the sparrow were always together...

But then it got colder. After autumn came winter. It was freezing and the land was white with snow.

Menno hid sadly under the roof tiles of the barn. Where was Pintail, his best friend? He had suddenly disappeared. He hadn't shown up on a cold day. Menno felt terribly alone. He flew over the white world every day, looking for food and...looking for Pintail!

"Pintail! Swallow! Where are you?" he kept chirping.

There was never an answer.

He had thick plumage to keep warm and the wind couldn't get under the tiles, yet the sparrow often shivered in his sleep when he dreamed of the merry swallow. When he woke up, he had tears in his little eyes...

It started to get warmer. It was spring! The snow disappeared, the meadow was full of colourful flowers and insects were buzzing everywhere. Menno sat there in the sun. What a beautiful day this was! Really a day to go out with Pintail! No, he still hadn't forgotten him. What did he suddenly hear there? Did someone call his name? That voice! That was Pintail! He wasn't dreaming, was he... in broad daylight?

"Hello, Menno! Here I am again!"

"Pigtail! You're back! Oh, how I have missed you! Where have you been all this time?"

"Swallows migrate to warm countries when it starts wintering here," Pintail explained. "Sparrows stay at home, swallows take off – towards the sun! But now I'll stay here again for a long time, with you... Come on, Menno! Let's go… Up to new adventures!"

The swallow spread its wings. He didn't fly too fast, so the sparrow could easily keep up with him. They were back together, the two friends!

"Let the winter stay away for a very long time!" cried Menno to Pintail. "If you only knew how happy I am to see you again!"

"I'm happy too," said Pintail. "I thought of you every day there in those distant lands."

If you ever see a swallow and a sparrow flying through the sky together, it will probably be the two best friends Menno and Pintail

In the zoo, a large space was set up for the penguins. They had their own pens there, a large field and a deep, fast-flowing stream that opened into a round pond.

They did not have to be bored there. Besides, if it was a quiet, gloomy day, they could always ask old penguin Polo if he told another tall tale. This penguin always had something to say.

"I was brought here because I broke my leg when I had to run from a polar bear," he used to say.

And then he told about great adventures, icy cold, long journeys and special encounters. Actually, no penguin in the zoo believed him, but it was so nice and cosy to listen to him.

One day a clever penguin asked:

"Polo, how could you have run from a polar bear? Penguins live at the South Pole and polar bears at the North Pole— the whole world is in between!"

Everyone laughed. He had told Polo the plain truth!

"Let me tell you something, dummy," said Polo, and immediately everyone knew that another strong story would follow.

"I was found as a chicken at the South Pole by a sailor. He took me aboard a great iron ship! We sailed across the oceans and also ended up at the North Pole. We went ashore— well, we entered a cold, white world. Very nice! And infinitely large! The skipper discovered a little polar bear, howling with hunger and covered by a thick layer of snow. He took the bear in his arms and went back to the ship. Suddenly a ferocious polar bear appeared, the size of an ocean liner! An angry giant, who tolerated no intruders in his territory.

"Run, Polo! Run!" cried the skipper.

He made it to the boat and quickly went up the gangplank. I tripped and broke my leg. Just before the ferocious polar bear could grab me, a sailor brought me aboard. I remember it all well. The little polar bear was named Rob. Don't ask me where he went... I kept having trouble with a limp and ended up here... So you can see that I really went to the North Pole."

The penguins laughed. It was a beautiful story, but they didn't believe a word of it.

A day later, a truck drove through the zoo. It was full of cages that contained polar bears. They moved to another part of the zoo. The penguins stood in a long line side by side, watching the truck. A large polar bear stared at them. Then his eyes suddenly became very large, and he exclaimed in astonishment:

"You there! Old Penguin! Is your name… Polo?"

"That's what I've been called all my life," Polo agreed. "Who's asking?"

"I... Rob the polar bear! Yeah, this is a surprise for both of us, isn't it? I've lived in the same zoo as you for years... and now we can see each other for a little while! This is so nice! Goodbye old friend! I will never forget that we sailed together on the same ship!"

"Goodbye, Rob! Goodbye, big friend!" cried Polo. "Maybe we'll see each other again! What a giant you have become! Goodbye!"

From that day on, the other penguins looked at old Polo with different eyes.

His tall tales turned out to be...true!

He had actually travelled from the South Pole to the North Pole on a ship!

LITTLE JASPER, THE WOODCUTTER'S SON

L ong, long ago, a woodcutter lived on the edge of a large, dark forest. He had built his own house of sturdy planks. The house stood between two old oak trees and the branches grew well above the roof. In the beginning, the woodcutter did good business. He could even buy a horse so that he could take the chopped wood to the city every week, where people queued to buy it from him – especially in winter everyone wanted firewood for the fireplace.

But one day, Ferdinand, as the woodcutter was called, fell ill and had to stay in bed. His son, little Jasper, climbed on the back of the workhorse and went into town to fetch a doctor. The doctor followed him in his own carriage and went into the wooden house to examine Ferdinand.

"You'll get better, Ferdinand, I'll give you the right medicine," said the doctor. "Keep in mind that it can take a very long time. You are absolutely not allowed to exert yourself in the coming months, so you can forget about chopping wood! Stay in bed as much as possible and you should also eat well every day. Then it will all come together again."

Now Jasper had to take care of everything. He cleaned up the house, took care of the meals, and put the workhorse in the stable every night.

Jasper also took an axe from his father and went into the woods to chop wood. But he was far from strong enough to fell thick trees.

"You don't have to work so hard, Jasper," said Ferdinand. "When I'm well again, I'll work with double effort and supply the whole city with firewood."

But meanwhile, the woodcutter stayed in bed and the supply of food ran out. Money stopped coming in… The future looked bleak for the man and his little son…

Jasper loved the forest and all the animals he saw there.

When he took the big workhorse to the meadow, he first had to walk a long way through the woods. He would let the horse graze and then sit on the fence himself— listen to the birds singing and look around.

The animals got used to his presence.

Crows became so tame that they sat next to him on the fence. Sometimes one even landed on his shoulder. In the cold winter, he brought pieces of bread to the meadow and fed the birds. Jasper loved the animals and the animals loved Jasper. He took home an old weasel with half-frozen paws to take care of. He put chickens that had fallen from the tree back into their nests. He, one day, freed a deer that had become entangled with its antlers in the bushes and brought stray toads back to their pool deep in the forest. He took care of a bird of prey with a broken wing until it could fly again.

"You are so good to the animals of the forest," his father often said, "that one day they will reward you too!"

Then Jasper shrugged.

"That's not necessary, is it, father? That's not necessary at all. I like to help the animals."

Sometimes the barn next to the wooden house looked like an animal hospital! Jasper quickly learned how to care for sick animals. Once he had even helped a little deer and in the barn were cages with birds, mice and lizards. As soon as the animals felt well again, he released them.

Now Jasper had other concerns on his mind.

His father was ill, food ran out, there was no money left in the house, he was unable to chop wood and the doctor's medicine had long since run out.

"You must sell the workhorse, Jasper," his father said one day. "There is no alternative. I have to eat well. Isn't that what the doctor said? There must be new drugs. It's getting cold and you're wearing your old, worn-out clothes. You'll catch a cold if you don't buy a warm jacket and new pants. Go to town tomorrow. Take our dearest workhorse and sell it. Bring me the money. Then we can decide together what to spend it on."

Jasper understood. His father had to have food and medicine. And it was true, his clothes were torn; there were even holes in his shoes. But selling the workhorse? The faithful horse that always pulled the cart of wood to the city?

He shook his head.

"No…" he whispered. "That sweet horse must not be sold…"

However, there seemed not to be any alternative. The next day he would go to town with the horse. Money was very much needed!

Jasper slept badly that night. He kept thinking about the horse, about his sick father and about their lack of everything…

Early in the morning, he prepared breakfast for his father. He cooked porridge from the last bit of oats left. He himself took an old sandwich with him when he went to the stable to fetch the horse.

"Sell the horse for a good price, boy!" he heard his father calling. "We desperately need the money!"

"Yes, father!" he shouted back.

Before going into town, he took the horse along the forest path to the meadow.

"First you have to graze a bit," he said. "Eat a lot of the tender grass that grows here. That's good for you…"

He climbed the fence, looked at the horse and… then a tear rolled down his cheek. How miserable he felt! Why could not he avoid having to sell the horse? If only there was money! Then he could buy food and get the right medicine from the doctor, then everything would be all right.

A crow came and sat next to him on the fence. Jasper had not even taken a bite of the old bread. He crumbled a piece on his hand and held it out to the crow. Gratefully, the bird picked up the crumbs. More crows arrived. Soon the boy had given them all his bread. Now he had nothing of his own.

"Never mind," he thought grimly, rubbing his eyes with his fingers. "I'm not hungry anyway. I can't get a bite down my throat!"

It was time to go to town.

Suddenly Jasper remembered his father's words:

"You are so good to the animals of the forest that they will reward you one day!"

If only that could be true!

He exclaimed in despair:

"Please, dear animals of the forest… please, help me! Yes, now I need your help!"

Startled, the crows flew away.

Nothing else happened. Jasper understood that. No one could help him now!

No one..?

He stared at the horse. Suddenly something moved in the grass in the meadow. The ground was pushed up. Jasper knew immediately why. A mole was digging a tunnel and pushing the earth away. In a short time, a molehill was formed. He had seen this so many times before. But what did he see now?

Something glittered among the loose earth.

His attention was immediately aroused.

He jumped off the fence and ran to the meadow.

He bent down by the molehill and picked up two large, shiny gold coins!

"Hurrah!" the boy exclaimed. "Gold! Real gold! Father and I have never seen anything but copper coins and this is pure gold!"

He jumped on the horse's back. A moment later he was on his way to town. He bought a few baskets full of food and new clothes for his father and for himself. He also went to the doctor for medicine and did not forget to buy his father a new, thick blanket. He returned home heavily laden…

He explained everything to his father.

"You see? You see, son?" exclaimed his father. "Now the animals have rewarded you for all your attention, for all your goodness! They paid you in gold because you always treated them so well…"

That evening there was a party in the wooden house. Ferdinand got out of bed and helped his son prepare a sumptuous meal.

ooo

The woodcutter now quickly got better. He was soon able to go back to work. Everything went back to the way it used to be. And one day Ferdinand said to his son:

"Come on, Jasper, let's go to the meadow. I want to see where the mole pushed the earth up."

Together they crossed the forest path. Ferdinand opened the gate. Jasper pointed to the spot where the molehill had been. Now grass grew there again.

"Moles have no money, moles have no gold, you understand that," said Ferdinand.

Jasper nodded.

"But where did those gold coins come from, father?"

Ferdinand had brought a spade and started digging.

"You know, boy," he said, "sometimes when the times are tumultuous, when there is rebellion or war, people get scared."

"I understand, father. I would also be afraid…"

"Rich people don't want to lose their money. They bury their coins and wait until the times are favourable again. But sometimes those same people move away when the ground gets too hot under their feet. They flee their home… they forget where they once hid their valuables. And look! Jasper, look here..!"

Ferdinand had plunged the spade deep into the hole he had already dug, and now he threw a stone pitcher into the grass. The pitcher was cracked. Gold coins rolled out… There were a lot of them!

"A forgotten treasure. Coins hidden under the ground… in a jar!" laughed Ferdinand. "When the mole dug its tunnel, it must have crawled past the jar. Two gold coins were pushed up. That's how you found them. And now, Jasper… we have a hundred gold coins! Maybe there are two hundred!"

Jasper started to cheer.

"Hurrah! Father! We are rich!"

OOO

Many years later, the old woodcutter and his son still lived in the same place. But the wooden house had been demolished and now there was a large brick house. Jasper was married and now had children of his own. He had spent the money well. He had gone to town and studied there. That is how he became an animal doctor. Jasper was very happy. He took care of sick animals and always knew how to make them better. His father no longer had to work. Old Ferdinand helped take care of all the animals that were kept in cages and pens in a huge barn.

"We owe this all to a mole that dug a corridor in the meadow where our workhorse grazed," Jasper explained to his children. "The mole made us rich, the mole made us happy…"

But when old Ferdinand heard that, he shook his head and said to his grandchildren:

"That's not quite true. I think it's all very different. When your father was a little boy, he helped all the animals. I used to say to him,

"Son, you're so good to the animals of the forest, they'll reward you one day!" Then the mole found the treasure and all the animals agreed that the gold coins should be for Jasper. Oh, if you only knew how proud I am of him!"

Well, Jasper and his family lived happily ever after… and all the animals cared for by doctor Jasper quickly recovered!

Jasper was rewarded… by all the animals of the forest…

THE BIG BEAVER BROOK IN THE FOREST

I t was very busy in the big brook in the woods.
The beavers were busy!

Beavers like calm water to live in, so they build a large dam.

The dam stops the rapidly streaming water of the brook and creates a large lake in which everyone— frogs, salamanders, toads, fish and of course the beavers themselves— can live happily.

Crack! Crack! Everywhere the big beavers were busy gnawing trees. Other beavers dragged the trees through the forest to the brook. There, all the trunks were tied together with small, flexible twigs. It would not be long before the dam in the creek was finished.

Little beaver Bongo was pushed away by a large beaver.

"Watch out, boy," he said, "we're all in a hurry and you're just getting in the way here. You are still much too small to help."

Bongo dribbled to the edge of the woods and looked at the stream. He saw all those big beavers working there as hard as they could! With large sticks and twigs, they dived into the water and on top of the new dam, the beaver boss stood giving directions.

"Quick!" he heard him shout, "we need another big tree trunk and on the other side a hole still has to be closed. There is still water seeping through and that is not allowed. Hurry up, because there is going to be a storm and if the dam is not strong enough, it will fall apart!"

The beavers worked as hard as they could and all over the woods fell over small trees they had gnawed with their strong teeth. They helped each other well. Two beavers were collecting clay. They scooped everything onto the large tails of two other beavers who then carefully went into the brook with their tails above the water. At the dam, the clay was removed and there the mason beavers closed the holes neatly.

The wind started blowing and dark clouds floated across the sky.

Moments later, the first drops fell…

"Faster! Faster!" cried the beaver boss. "We need to have many more branches and also some little tree trunks. Come on friends, keep going! If we do it fast enough, we will succeed!"

Little beaver Bongo walked deeper into the forest, lost in thought. He wasn't paying attention and bumped into a thin, tall tree. Ouch, that hurt! Bongo looked up. What a beautiful tree that was. A real tree to strengthen the dam with.

But what did the great beavers always say to him?

Oh yes, he was still too small to help. He just got in the way.

Well, there was no one to be seen here, so he could not get in anyone's way. He looked one more time at the tree and then he muttered:

"I'm going to gnaw down that tree. After all, I have to learn that if I want to become a big, well-working beaver?"

Bongo liked being a little beaver and he dreamt of growing up and being able to help build such a beautiful dam.

In the meantime, the wind had grown stronger and it had now started to rain. That was of course not a problem for the beavers themselves because these rodents love water. But all that rain could be a problem for the new dam that was not yet finished. If it collapsed, all the work would have been for nothing!

Bongo set his teeth in the tree trunk.

The wood was hard. How did those big beavers manage to just gnaw down all those trees? He bit again and now a bit of bark and wood fell to the ground. Well, that was a start...

"Friends, can it really not work faster?" he heard the beaver boss shout above the howling wind. "Look there! The dam begins to break. Water is already coming through! Over here, you, with that big tree. And we need much more clay! Quick!"

Now everyone was helping. Even the little beavers made themselves useful. They began to dig in the ground and load the tails of the great beavers with earth.

"Where's Bongo?" he heard someone calling. "He may be the smallest of all the little beavers… but he can come and help us too, right?"

But Bongo stayed where he was and began to gnaw with double strength. His jaws started to hurt. It was a good thing that he had always been aware of how the great beavers worked, and he persevered with determination.

It was storming now! He felt the cold wind in his fur. When he looked behind him, he couldn't see the stream anymore because of the heavy rain. All around the bushes, he heard the rustling of leaves– the beavers were gathering twigs to fill the gaps in the dam.

Now he looked at his own tree. Half the work was already done. He never knew he had such sharp teeth and strong jaws. He started to get tired, but he kept going. Gnaw, gnaw! More and more pieces of wood fell to the ground and formed a mound.

"We're not going to make it, beaver boss!" someone shouted. "We are still missing a lot! There must be a big tree in the middle of the dam to strengthen everything. But who can gnaw down a tree so quickly?"

The beaver boss sat down on the dam defeated… What could he do now? Everyone did their very best. The dam cracked and the beaver boss almost fell over! The storm drove waves against the dam that washed away the wet clay.

Again and again a large beaver jumped into the water with a few twigs between its teeth. The twigs were taken by other beavers and they braided them into the dam. But no, it didn't help much…

"A tree trunk!" exclaimed the beaver boss in despair. "Let three or four strong beavers gnaw down a tree, and maybe we'll make it. But then it has to be done very quickly!"

Four beavers clambered to the side and began to gnaw on the first tree they could find. The wind howled through the branches, the rain poured down.

"Hurry up! Hurry up!"

But the beavers could not do any faster.

A high wave, pushed up by the still-increasing storm, swept over the dam and the beaver boss was flung into the water. The dam cracked and shook horribly. The four beavers looked up from their work and realized that they could never gnaw their tree in time again.

Splash!

A little beaver dove into the water. And what did that brave animal have in its mouth?

"A tree trunk!" everyone shouted. "Look what a big trunk! Exactly what we need! Little beaver Bongo has gnawed it down! Let's help him quickly, then we will be able to save the dam after all!"

The four big beavers dived after him, grabbed the branches between their teeth and swam as fast as they could to the dam. The beaver boss had climbed on it again and gave directions.

"It's going well, friends! Push the branches in between, keep the trunk straight and secure it with twigs! Throw lots of clay on it, yes… that will do!"

Then everyone started cheering.

It worked! Now it was allowed to storm and rain even harder. The dam was strong enough.

The beaver boss lifted Bongo out of the water.

"Come and stand next to me," he said. "You saved our dam! Tomorrow it will be another beautiful, sunny day and then we will celebrate. I'll make sure you get the tastiest snacks!"

"So I didn't get in the way?" asked Bongo shyly.

"Walked in the way?" repeated the beaver boss in astonishment. "No! Of course not! How do you get to that? Today you were the best worker!"

And to show that they agreed with the beaver boss, all the big beavers slapped their tails on the water. Bongo was very happy about that because when beavers do that, it means exactly the same as when people clap their hands.

You don't often get that much applause, especially if you're just a little beaver...

THE LITTLE KNIGHT

12

It was not the best day for Knight Arthur. For even though he was safe by the fire in the great hall, outside the Black Knight and his men had surrounded the castle. What could he do? The Black Knight was the terror of the neighbourhood. Everywhere he went he wanted to boss about and no one dared to challenge him. He had already conquered all the castles in the area.

The Black Knight was a big, tall man who had mastered the art of sword fighting and had never lost a fight—his black armour didn't show the slightest scratch.

Anyone who met him immediately ran away.

Knight Arthur was not a scary person at all. But he was not strong. He was small. In fact, he was so small that he rode a donkey instead of a horse. How could a little knight like him ever compete against that great Black Knight?

Arthur's father had been a very big man. Even bigger than the Black Knight! You could still tell by his armour, which stood in the armoury among the spears, swords, axes and shields. Of course, his father had hoped that Arthur would grow as strong as himself. But when he understood that Arthur would always be a little knight, he had said again and again:

"Arthur, who is not strong must be smart. Never forget about that!"

Meanwhile, the castle was under siege and no one knew what to do next to turn the tide.

The soldiers of the castle sat chattering behind the battlements and even the horses were shivering in the stable.

"Hello there, Arthur… little knight! Come out, if you dare!"

The Black Knight's black voice could be heard throughout the castle.

"If you don't come out, I'll come in. I'll break open the gate! I don't intend to wait much longer, because it's cold here and I can see from the smoke coming from your chimney that the fire is burning. Soon your castle will be mine, little one!"

Arthur got very angry. That evil Black Knight had been making the area unsafe for months now and that had to end. But then… how could a little knight like him do something about that?

"He who is not strong must be smart!"

Of course! That was it! He'd give that Black Knight a good scare. He would scare him so much that he would never come back…

　　　　　CHILDREN'S SHORT STORIES

For though Arthur was but a little knight, he certainly was not afraid!

He got up and walked to the courtyard of his castle.

"Soldiers," he said, "go to the kitchen. There is a large kettle of soup ready and there is fresh bread. You don't have to keep watch anymore…"

"My dear…Oh no…" sighed one of the soldiers, "that doesn't mean you give the castle to the Black Knight, does it? When he comes in, he immediately slurps that soup kettle empty and from then on we have to do what he says from early morning until late evening!"

The soldiers left their posts and sauntered in. They wondered what Arthur was going to do next.

Well, Arthur went to his blacksmith and said:

"Walk with me to the armoury, you must help me."

The blacksmith was just making a small sword for Arthur. It didn't seem much bigger than a dagger… He left the work behind and went with the knight.

In the armoury, Arthur said:

"Look at my father's gigantic armour!"

The blacksmith heaved a deep sigh.

"Well, if there were a knight who would fit into that great suit of armour, the Black Knight wouldn't dare show himself here much longer, I'm sure of that!"

"Precisely! You're absolutely right," grinned Arthur. "That armour is so huge... and no one can see who's in it..."

The blacksmith did not understand the remark.

But Arthur continued:

"Help me get into that harness. After that, you need to close the helmet visor. Then suddenly I am the greatest knight in the land…"

Now the blacksmith understood and he clapped his hands enthusiastically.

"This is a clever plan…"

He began to help the knight. It didn't take long for Arthur to disappear into the armour. It was very difficult to walk around in that heavy armour, but if he tried hard, he could make good strides.

The armour jingled loudly with every movement as Arthur went to the gate. In one hand he held one of his father's huge swords. It was so heavy that the point dragged over the boulders.

"Black Knight!" cried Arthur in a deep voice. "I've given you long enough to disappear. Now I'm coming out!"

The Black Knight burst out laughing and his soldiers roared with him.

"Bring it on! Who are you that you dare to take on me?"

The blacksmith pushed open the gate. Arthur had to use all his strength to move forward in that huge armour. He went through the gate and over the drawbridge.

"Those who are not strong must be smart," he thought with each difficult step, "who are not strong must be smart, those who are not strong…"

Soon everyone would be able to see him…

"Well?" cried the Black Knight. "Where are you, braggart?"

He looked at the drawbridge and the gate and expected little Arthur to show up with his little sword.

But… what did he see there? No, that couldn't be Arthur! There was a giant! No one had ever seen such a large, imposing knight. The soldiers hid behind their shields and slowly backed away.

The Black Knight was no longer smiling. He stood there, his teeth chattering, shaking so much that his metal arms clattered against his metal breastplate.

"Come here and fight!" said Arthur, again in a deep voice.

The Black Knight threw his sword away from him and ran. His metal legs made a grinding noise. He rushed after his soldiers.

Arthur laughed and felt relieved. Fortunately, everything had gone quickly, because he was so tired of walking in that heavy armour that he could hardly move a step. His father's sword fell from his hand...

The blacksmith was already there, helping him out of the armour.

"Will you come with me?" asked the blacksmith. "You have won the battle and there is still hot soup in the kitchen… And though you are small… by all accounts you are the greatest knight in the land – and most certainly the bravest!"

The large armour is still in the armoury and it is carefully cleaned every day. And when another knight appears who thinks he can beat Arthur, he can count on that giant knight to come out through the gate and over the drawbridge again…

13

CONJURER OR WIZARD

There is a big difference between a conjurer and a wizard. A conjurer is handy and knows enough tricks to make you believe that everything he does is real. Nimble-fingered as he is, he may make you believe he made a coin disappear when in reality he quickly slipped it up his sleeve. A wizard can really make anything disappear. But yes, it is said that wizards don't actually exist.

But what can we say about the Great Boris? For years he travelled the world and amazed people with his tricks. He conjured all sorts of things out of his top hat. And he never told anyone exactly how he managed that. He later retired and hung his top hat on the hat stand. People wanted to have a petting zoo in his hometown, but there was not enough money for that.

Big Boris had become a rich man and bought a piece of land on which he build a farm. When the children were allowed to visit for the first time, they saw pens and meadows full of animals! There were sheep, rabbits, hamsters, pigs, chickens, goats and pigeons. Admission to the petting zoo was free and from that day on it was crowded.

Parents took their children there and they all had a great time. Then the mayor and the aldermen decided that a major road had to be built that would run right through the land on which the petting zoo was built. That same day, Big Boris was spotted near the petting zoo and... it soon turned out that all the animals had disappeared!

No trucks had come to take them, and yet they were gone now.

The kids hated it! An empty petting zoo! Together with their parents, they went to the town hall to have a word with the mayor and the aldermen. They came out and went to take a look at the petting zoo themselves. They were shocked by all those empty pens and deserted meadows.

"That road can also be built elsewhere," the mayor concluded. "I'll go to Big Boris and ask him to bring the animals back."

Everyone was happy. The people all went to Boris' house and the mayor rang the bell. Boris came out. He had removed his top hat from the hat stand. In a long procession, they went to the petting zoo and there the people got to see something that they still can't believe! At every pen and meadow, Big Boris would stop and put his hand into the top hat. Again and again, he took out animals; the sheep, rabbits, hamsters, pigs, chickens, goats and pigeons were back! Then Big Boris put the hat on his head and walked back home, hands in pockets and nose in the air.

Was he a conjurer? Or a real wizard? No one can tell for sure. It is true that the petting zoo is still there and that all the animals that live there are doing well...

One day a journalist from the local newspaper went to ask Big Boris. But Boris's answer was not very clear.

"It doesn't matter if I'm a conjurer or a wizard," he told the journalist. "It's about the animals having a good time and that the children can visit them again."

That was all the journalist could tell about it in the paper...

14

THE ADVENTURE OF THE CROW

The Jansen family was away for a week. Father, mother and the two children were on vacation. The house was well locked and the neighbours would keep an eye on it. What happened that week, no one could have predicted! Kobus the crow lived nearby and had been looking for a suitable place to build a new nest for some time.

Searching he flew back and forth and suddenly he noticed the chimney on the roof of the Jansen family. It had only recently been placed there, because Mr. Jansen had had a fireplace built in the living room. Kobus sat on the edge of the chimney pipe and stared down. It was pitch dark in the chimney. Was this a suitable place to build a best? He wanted to find out and he pushed off with his feet and dived into the chimney. Kobus fell straight down. The chimney was too narrow for him to spread his wings. So a moment later he sat in the ashes of the fireplace and looked around bewildered. He tried to go up the chimney again, flapping his wings, but he couldn't. Ash and soot flew around and made the living room dirty. In a panic, Kobus began to fly back and forth. He nearly bumped into the lamp, threw books and figurines from a cupboard, shattered a flower vase and flew his beak against the large window.

Kobus got angry. He wanted to get out of here! Making a cawing sound, he started flying all over the house, throwing things on the floor everywhere. In the kitchen he broke cups and plates, in the bedrooms, he tore posters from the walls and threw the children's toys out of the cupboards. It was as if a tornado had gone through the house! Back in the living room, he pushed the telephone off a table with his beak. He sat down on a chair by the dining table and fluttered his wings until the furniture tipped over. Framed photos ended up on the floor. A stone piggy bank shattered and more than a hundred coins rolled in all directions.

Kobus was still furious.

Finally, he flew up two flights of stairs and ended up in the attic. There was a window ajar. With great difficulty he managed to squeeze through and then, at last, the crow was free again! He flew through the air, cawing loudly, and then he began to feel a little calmer again.

The Jansen family was very surprised when they came home to find that havoc. How could all this have happened?

The neighbours had seen nothing and nobody. All doors were locked properly. And yet everything in the house had been knocked over and smashed to pieces. The police were called in and they too could not find out what had been the cause of so much mess. So

　　　　　　　　　　　　　　CHILDREN'S SHORT STORIES

the family had no choice but to clean up quickly. In the evening the four of them sat by the fireplace. Father put a few pieces of wood in the hearth and struck a match. Suddenly he saw something lying there. He picked it up.

"A black feather," he muttered. "How does he get here?"

No one could answer that. Mother took the feather from him and put it in a vase.

"Beautiful," she said. "It must be a crow's feather."

Moments later, the fireplace was burning and no one wondered how the feather got into the house. It has always remained a mystery to the Jansen family how the havoc in their house could have started.

And Kobus the crow? He later built a nest under the roof tiles of an old house and never returned to the roof of the Jansen family...

15

THE NICEST SNAKES IN THE FOREST

It was so hot in the tropical forest that even the capybaras were puffing from the heat. And they were still up to their necks in water…

Day in, day out, the sun shone down on the trees and bushes. The wood became bone dry and some plants turned completely brown instead of green because the roots couldn't find water. No, it had rarely been this hot.

The animals looked at each other confused. What was going on?

An old parrot screeched: "Something strange is going to happen, I'm sure of it. If only I knew what it was…"

The parrots sitting in the same tree with him shrugged.

"We don't know either. But something is going on, we agree with you, that's for sure!"

They had sat under the canopy of leaves in the shade, because the sun was too hot for them too.

"Look!" cried one of the birds. "Here comes my cousin flying in. I hope he can tell us more…"

Cousin parrot perched on a branch and said:

"Everyone needs to be warned. There was a hunter near my tree. He smoked a cigar and threw the burning butt on the floor. The grass was so dry that a fire broke out immediately. It won't be long before everything burns here too! Get out of here!"

He himself set the example by flying away again and shouting:

"Alarm! Fire! Fire! Everybody get out of here!"

The other parrots flew away too, high above the trees. When they looked back, they saw thick clouds of smoke approaching.

"Fire!" they screeched now too. "Anyone who cannot fly must flee! Get in the water! There is a fire! That's why it feels even hotter here than usual!"

All the animals that heard it immediately ran. The birds showed the way, the animals that could not fly ran after them. But the fire was fast approaching! Oh, wat a stupid, stupid hunter that was! Making a fire in such a bone-dry forest… smoking a cigar! Such a blockhead!

Now the strangest animals appeared. An armadillo trotted through the bushes. It looked like a knight in armour. Two jaguars, one spotted and one inky black, ran past a small deer. They did not think of chasing the deer now. They just shouted:

"Walk after us, we know a way to avoid the fire!"

And the little one did his very best to keep up with the two predators. It worked out well, because deer can make big jumps!

All the animals moved in the same direction, in the opposite direction of the approaching fire.

It looked like they might be able to escape the fire, but suddenly they couldn't go any further…

A chasm twelve feet wide barred their way. The deer looked carefully over the edge. The gorge turned out to be staggeringly deep. No, no one dared to jump over it. The parrots circled above the animals:

"You must get to the other side as soon as possible! The fire is everywhere now. If you stay here, the flames will reach you!"

The two jaguars looked at each other anxiously.

"If I take a good running start and don't look down, I might make it," said the inky predator.

"Yes, maybe…maybe," muttered the spotted one. "I'll make it, I think. But what about all the other animals? What about the little deer, with the sloth and the armadillo? What about the little monkeys and the mice? If only we could come up with something…"

"Yes, but make it up quickly!" screeched the parrots, high from the safety of the sky.

Soot particles were already swirling through the air and the smoke was seeping into everyone's nostrils. The animals started to get very nervous.

The little deer ran in panic and wanted to jump. But no… it stopped just in time. The animals huddled together in fear and no one knew what to do next.

Until… two big snakes crawled up!

They were both about fifteen feet long and they looked exactly alike. They were the twins Sisser and Blazer and no one had ever wanted anything to do with those two. But now things were suddenly very different…

Sisser and Blazer looked at the deep chasm and then they looked at each other.

"Do you understand what we should do now, brother?" one asked.

"Of course, brother, I understand that very well," hissed the other.

Side by side they moved to the edge of the deep chasm. The animals wondered what those two were up to. With a few quick movements of their lithe snake bodies, the two large snakes suddenly swept across the chasm!

Together they formed a bridge.

An escape route!

This was a great plan!

"Hurry up, everyone!" hissed Sisser. "The fire is almost here and everyone still has to get across!"

"Hurry up!" said Blazer. "And please walk carefully. Quick, we won't last too long, as you will understand!"

The fire was already so close that the animals could hear the wood snapping in the flames.

The deer was the first to cross. It carefully placed its hooves on the skin of the snakes and walked across the gorge.

"Hurry up!" screeched the parrots.

Fortunately, more large snakes then appeared and they did the same as the friendly twins. They were the nicest snakes in the tropical forest! Together they formed bridges that spanned the gorge.

The monkeys swung lithely past the snakes to the other side and the jaguars did it one step at a time. Who would have ever thought that those big, dangerous snakes could be so helpful! They all held on bravely and didn't make a sound when the bigger, heavier animals stamped on them too.

In the end, everyone made it to the other side safely. There the animals stood in amazement, watching the fire.

"Noe we have to say goodbye to our dear forest," sighed the black jaguar. "All because of such a stupid, smoking hunter!"

The snakes now also wriggled to the other side. They were in pain in their long bodies, but were very happy that everyone had made it.

The animals clapped and stamped their hooves, and the deer danced merrily about.

"Thank you on behalf of all of us," said an armadillo. "For oh, if it hadn't been for you, everything would have turned out to be a great disaster!"

Sisser and Blazer looked at each other.

"Who would have ever thought something like this should happen," Blazer hissed. "We formed a strong bridge together and let all the animals walk all over us!"

And Sisser said: "That's how we managed to save everyone. It only left me with a bit of pain in the back…"

Together they wriggled away to explore their new habitat.

All the other animals followed them, into a new future…

THE SQUIRREL AND THE WOODPECKER

The tree, which stood in the middle of the large clearing in the forest, actually looked like a tower block. All kinds of animals lived above and below each other. At the very bottom, among the thick roots, a fox had dug its den. A little higher, against the trunk, the forester had attached two wooden houses. In one lived a stately robin family and in the other a noisy sparrow family. At the very top of the branches, there were also birds, but they had all even built their nests. And of course, there were all kinds of animals that are so small that you can hardly see them; beetles, cockroaches, earwigs and spiders.

Near the fox's lair was even a huge anthill that housed countless ants.

Yet there was still enough room in the branches and the trunk of the tree for new inhabitants. For example, bird nests could still be added.

On the highest branch of the tree sat a strange little bird.

It had all kinds of colours and a pointed beak. It was a woodpecker. He had heard that there must be a hole in the trunk of this mighty tree. Woodpeckers like to live in trees, so this one thought:

"Who knows, I might turn it into a nice house, I'll take a look."

Woodpeckers are able to climb quickly up and down a tree trunk and now this one did too, looking for an opening.

"Where can it be?"

Then he found it. Yes, maybe this was an ideal place to live… When he was almost there, he saw a squirrel running up the trunk. It was a beautiful squirrel with a thick, long tail. And… he too went straight for the hole in the tree.

The woodpecker now used its wings to move faster and… boom! There the squirrel and the woodpecker, right in front of the hole in the tree trunk, collided with their heads.

"Excuse me," said the squirrel politely, "I'd like to see this nest and…"

"Me too," said the woodpecker. "I want to live here."

"That was my intention," said the squirrel. "What do we do now? Because we know we are both equally entitled to it… we arrived here at exactly the same time."

The woodpecker thought it over. Finally, he said:

"I have an idea. We take turns giving each other a riddle. Whoever gives an incorrect answer loses the game and the winner gets to live here. What do you say to that?"

The squirrel agreed and the woodpecker was allowed to start.

"It has four legs, a tail and it can bark, what could that be?"

"Uh… well… a dog!" the squirrel responded.

That was a good answer, so now he got to give a riddle.

"It's white and it's in a bottle."

"Uh… milk!"

It was the woodpecker's turn again.

"When you look into it, you see yourself. What is that?"

The squirrel knew that.

"A mirror."

To rest, they both went inside, as it became a little difficult to talk as they had to hold on to the bark of the tree. It was a spacious two-story den and everything was neatly tidied; the previous occupants had left it tidy.

The squirrel said:

"What do you order at the bakery on someone's birthday?"

"Pastry," said the woodpecker, and immediately went on:

"What comes after spring?"

"The summer…"

And so they went on. Hour after hour! Whatever the woodpecker asked, the squirrel always gave the correct answer. Whatever the squirrel came up with, the woodpecker always knew what it was all about. In the end, they both almost fell asleep, they had become so tired.

"I'm going to get some beechnuts because I'm getting hungry," said the squirrel. "I'll be right back."

He crawled out and the woodpecker immediately flew away to look for something to eat as well.

An hour later they were back together in the hole in the tree and again uttered riddle after riddle. Neither of them managed to ask a question that the other couldn't answer and so it happened that the woodpecker stayed overnight in the den and… the squirrel too!

The next morning, when the sun had just risen, they started again.

And… they still do, because there doesn't seem to be a riddle that the squirrel or the woodpecker can't solve!

Sometimes, when it is very quiet in the forest on a beautiful summer evening, you can see the fox coming out of its den and the birds sitting on the branches of the big tree. Rabbits, wild boars and even deer come to listen. And what do they hear? Then they hear how the squirrel and the woodpecker give each other riddles.

No one in the woods knows what will happen if one day one of those two doesn't know the right answer.

Although… everyone says that the squirrel and the woodpecker have become the best of friends…

17

THE DANCING KANGAROO

Tango the kangaroo always danced! He lived in a small meadow in the zoo. A high wooden fence had been erected around the meadow. Tango danced and jumped on his big hind legs and he always just got his head above the fence. He could see the cage across the path, in which an old brown bear spent his days. The old bear looked longingly at the gate each morning, waiting to see the merry head of the dancing kangaroo again.

"Hello!" it sounded, as soon as he saw Tango - and then he was already gone.

Immediately he reappeared above the edge of the fence: "Hello there, bear!" He was gone. And there he came again: "Did you sleep well?" The bear grunted with pleasure. Tango always made small talk this way and he loved it. His greatest wish was to see the kangaroo up close. Until now he had only been able to look at his head.

It was the middle of winter when something extraordinary happened. There was a stiff frost. Tango danced all day to keep warm. "Hello, bear! Cold! Cold!" The sky had turned grey. Snow began to fall. The storm arose. Never before has there been so much snow in one day. The world turned white. The zoo was closed! Hour after hour the snow fell. On one side, Tango's pasture bordered a shed with a pitched roof. The roof now creaked under the weight of a huge layer of snow. The storm swelled and suddenly all that snow slid down from the roof and ended up in Tango's pasture. Tango was completely covered with snow. He managed to work his way up with his big, strong hind legs.

There was now so much snow in the meadow that even the high fence was buried under it.

Cautiously, the kangaroo began to walk. He kept sinking deep into the snow, but he still made good progress. He went up a high mountain of snow, slid down the other side and... now he was out of the meadow! With great leaps, he crossed the snowy path and then he stopped in front of the old bear's cage.

The bear sat quietly in a corner watching the falling snowflakes.

"Hello, bear!" said Tango. "Now I finally have time for a nice chat. Now I don't have to jump and I don't have to say short sentences. I'll stand by the bars of your cage for a while, you know..."

The bear couldn't believe his ears and couldn't believe his eyes...

His jaw dropped and his dark beady eyes suddenly became very large.

"Tango! Finally, I can see you up close. Now I can watch you from head to toe! I didn't even know what a kangaroo looked like. Did you escape?"

The bear waddled toward the bars.

"I could walk out over a high mountain of snow."

The bear pushed his snout between the bars and Tango rubbed the old bear's nose.

"What is that, old bear? Do I see tears there?"

The bear let out a sob.

"It's so nice to see you, Tango. I'm a lonely bear and you make me happy every time by dancing and jumping near the fence, so I can at least see your face. You have no idea how happy I am that you are so close to me now."

All day long, Tango stayed near the bear's cage. The two animals told each other stories and had a lot of fun. It wasn't until the snow had stopped and they heard guards with snow shovels approaching in the distance that it was time to say goodbye.

Tango rubbed the bear's nose.

The bear said:

"Thank you, Tango. See you tomorrow! Then I'll see your face again above the fence, won't I?"

Tango nodded.

"You can always count on me. Bye, bear!"

The kangaroo walked over the snow hill back to his pasture. Moments later, the zookeepers had swept the snow everywhere.

Tango the kangaroo is still dancing in his meadow.

He jumps up and looks at the old bear's cage.

"Hello there, bear!"

"Hello there, Tango!"

"Are you all right, old bear?"

"You bet, Tango! Nice to see you again!"

The dancing kangaroo and the old bear are the best of friends.

And they will remain friends forever!

18

THE GOLDEN MAGIC LIZARD

It had been sweltering hot for days on end. The sun shone from a clear sky and scorched the land. It cooled down a little at night. The animals in the big forest hid as much as possible in the shade. The pools had dried up, there was no water anywhere. Only early in the morning, there were a few drops of dew on the withered leaves of the bushes.

"Maybe the golden magic lizard will come," an old fox said to the other animals one evening. "It is said that he only shows up when it has been so hot for a long time. He lives deep underground, but in hot summers he sometimes emerges."

He had made the other animals curious.

"Tell me more about the golden magic lizard!" insisted the deer, hares and squirrels.

They forgot the heat for a moment and sat in a circle around the fox.

"The golden magic lizard is very friendly. When he has crawled above the ground, he asks someone to make a wish. And then he makes that wish come true. A long time ago there was a squirrel who was allowed to make a wish."

Naturally, everyone wanted to know what the squirrel had asked for.

"He had pointed the golden magic lizard to a large hollow tree and asked if he would fill it with tasty nuts. That happened! The squirrel never had to look for food again and was never hungry again."

All the animals sighed deeply. That squirrel was lucky, they agreed.

"A frog was also allowed to make a wish. He wanted to move to a pond near a palace. It was immediately arranged for him and he got his own pond in a king's garden!"

The old fox also told of the last time, years ago, that the golden magic lizard had appeared.

"Now it was a magpie who was allowed to make a wish. He wanted to become wealthy. He got a huge nest with a golden roof, high in the branches of a silver tree. There are no leaves on that tree, but sparkling diamonds..."

The fox was silent. It was quiet again in the forest. Everyone thought about what he had said. The moon rose. It was midnight, but it was still warm. The animals were tired and very thirsty. By the light of the moon, they could see each other. Everyone was exhausted. It was just too hot to sleep well.

Something slipped down the trunk of a tree. There was a golden sparkle in the bright moonlight. A large lizard crept up to the animals. His scales and tail were of pure gold and his eyes glittered like gems.

"The golden magic lizard!" exclaimed the animals. "There he is! The old fox just told about you, lizard..."

The lizard stopped right in front of the old fox and said:

"Is that right? That is very nice. So I haven't been forgotten yet."

"Oh no, no…" said the old fox. "I've talked about you and told the animals about the wishes of the squirrel, the frog, and the magpie."

"Now another animal is allowed to make a wish," said the golden magic lizard. "You, old fox! You can say what you want and I'll make sure you get it. Then I disappear again... and maybe I'll come back in a few years. Tell me, old fox, what can I do for you?"

All the animals held their breath. What would they themselves wish if they stood in his place? A palace, a bag full of gold, a crown...? The old fox cocked his head, looked at the golden magic lizard and said:

"I already know, oh yes, I know exactly what I want! Rain! That's what we all need! Let it rain for the rest of the night and let it cool down a bit here! That is my wish!"

"Old fox, you are a noble animal," said the witch lizard. "You have not desired something for yourself, but you want something useful for everyone. I'm so happy about that. Your wish is fulfilled..."

A cloud passed over the moon! It became dark! The golden magic lizard had suddenly disappeared.

Then it started to rain!

The animals cheered and danced.

Rain! Rain! After all those days of heat and drought! It even snowed, it felt like winter. The animals rolled in the puddles and splashed each other wet. They drank from the pools that had appeared all over the forest. And they thanked the fox who had not only thought of himself but had made a wish that made everyone in the great forest happy.

The golden magic lizard did not show up again that year. Who knows, you might even run into him one day when you walk through the woods on a hot day...

19

E ach time at the end of the school year, the teacher would ask, "Where are you going on vacation?" Then the children shouted, "To Spain! To Italy! To Greece! To Germany!"

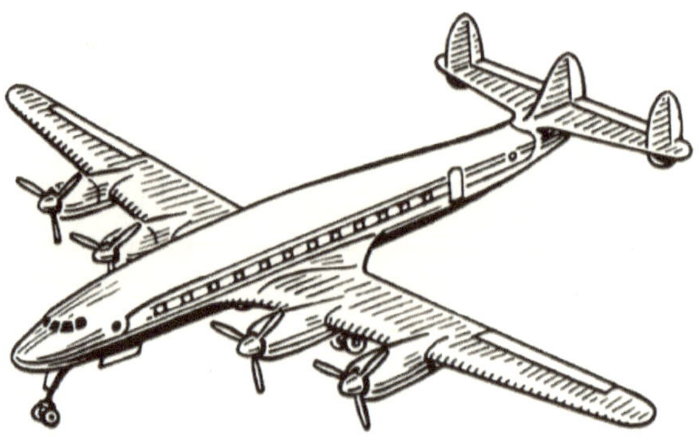

Little Johan Speck never said anything. There was no money at home to go on vacation. When everyone looked at him, it made him shy.

"Johan Speck will of course stay at home!" the children shouted and they began to laugh.

Johan dreamed of distant journeys and great adventures. But he was at home all day.

The holiday had just begun when the postman rang the bell early one morning. John opened it.

"Something incredible happened, little fellow," said the postman. "The carpenter was busy renovating the post office. He removed a wooden cabinet that has been there for nearly a hundred years.

And what do you think he found there? A letter! An ancient letter. It must have fallen behind the closet at some point. Look what is written on it."

He gave a yellowed and crumpled envelope to Jan, who saw in graceful handwriting on the front: "To Johan Speck, Village Street 20".

He didn't understand this...

He thanked the postman and went inside.

His mother opened the letter. She was just as surprised as he was.

"It's an invitation. From the new emperor of China! Johan Speck is invited to his party to attend the coronation!"

In the evening, when his father came home, it became clear what was going on.

"Your great-grandfather was also called Johan Speck and he was an important merchant," he explained. "The letter was written to your great-grandfather. How nice is this! I'm going to call the newspaper right away." That was a good idea. The next day it was already in the newspaper with big headlines:

"Story cold letter for Johan Speck from the Village Street".

But it didn't end there. The television thought it was an interesting subject and a camera crew came to Johan's house for an interview. It was broadcasted in the evening. The international press also liked it very much. The film was bought by television stations from other countries. And then, halfway through the big holiday, the postman rang the bell of Johan again:

"Oh-oh, you won't believe this, Johan… A letter from China. With a gold rim and the most beautiful stamps, I've ever seen. It's for you, Johan. Look.. here it is!"

His mother opened the letter and her eyes widened as she read its contents.

"The news of the old letter has reached the new emperor of China. He's throwing a big party in a week. Kings, queens, princes, princesses, ministers and many other important people have received an invitation. And... do you know who his guest of honour is? The young Johan Speck from the Village Street! You can fly to China and you will sleep in the palace! The young emperor would like to meet you and he hopes you and he will become good friends. Oh… and your father and I can come with you."

Johnny couldn't believe all this. An invitation from the Emperor of China! Of course, he never expected anything like this.

And then, after a few weeks, the big vacation was over and the kids went back to school.

"Tell me, where have you been on vacation?"

The children now first looked at Johan's beaming face.

"To Germany," a girl said softly. "It rained every day."

"We went to Spain," said a boy. "It was very hot this year. Actually too hot to go outside."

No one else opened his mouth.

"And you, Johan Speck?" the teacher asked.

A big grin appeared on Johan Speck's face. He sat up and said proudly:

"I received an invitation from the Emperor of China and I slept in the palace. We have become good friends and I am going there again next year."

The teacher burst out laughing.

　　　　CHILDREN'S SHORT STORIES

"You made that up nicely, boy, but of course, nobody believes anything about it."

"It's true sir! Really true!" all the children cried.

"Ah, stop it!" the teacher laughed. "Who would believe such a thing? Does a boy from Village Street just get an invitation from an emperor? I think you are just a dreamer, Johan..."

Johan bent down. His bag was on the floor next to his table. He produced a big photo album.

"Well, sir," he said, "if you really don't believe it, I'll show you the pictures!"

Everyone was allowed to view the photos.

Little Johan Speck was the hero of the school!

20

THE MUSICAL CAT

Have you ever heard a cat play the piano? Is that impossible? Or are you not sure, because you don't have a cat and piano yourself? Well, to be honest, not all cats can play the piano – we all know that, of course. And yet there was a cat…

Here is a special story…

Mr. Fred, a piano teacher, was a very absent-minded man. He couldn't remember anything. For example, even if he had to go buy a packet of sugar and a packet of salt, he would write it down on a piece of paper, otherwise, he would have forgotten what he wanted before he got to the store. And without that piece of paper he might, after much thought, have asked for a few kilos of potatoes and a bag of biscuits in the shop…

     CHILDREN'S SHORT STORIES

The neighbours were happy with him. Because he could play so beautifully! When he sat at the piano, the neighbours turned off the television or radio to listen to the beautiful music. For though he forgot almost everything, he never forgot how to play the piano!

One day he had to travel because he was invited to play with a large orchestra in a large concert hall abroad. He would be gone for a few days. He packed his suitcase, put on his coat and went to the bus stop. The bus would take him to the airport.

Well, of course, he had forgotten something. But what? No, it couldn't be his toothbrush or his fancy suit. No, this time it was about something completely different!

For the door and the windows of his little house were closed. And who was downstairs, in the living room, sleeping in his basket?

Exactly… Mr. Fred's cat!

Fred flew abroad and was kindly received there. The conductor of the orchestra took him out to dinner and later they went to the concert hall together to see the beautiful grand piano that Mr. Fred was allowed to play.

Fred had completely forgotten to set out enough food for the cat, nor had he told the neighbours that he would be absent for a week.

The neighbours did have a key, but because they didn't know he wasn't there, they didn't go in to look after the cat and the plants.

Poor cat…

At first, he didn't even realize that the piano teacher had left.

He only started to think it strange when he noticed that his water bowl had not been refilled and that no cat food had been put in the other bowl.

Two empty bowls...

That was annoying because the tomcat was hungry and thirsty.

The doors of all the lockers were closed.

Well, since the situation didn't change, he lay down on a chair and tried to sleep. Soon he dreamed of bowls full of food and clear water.

When he awoke it was already dark and Fred still wasn't home.

Somewhere in the kitchen was a small bowl of water. He began to drink voraciously. And then there was little he could do but go back to sleep… and so it finally became morning.

Still no food, still no Fred…

The cat jumped onto the windowsill and saw the neighbour get on his bike to go to work and his wife just drove away in her car.

"Meow!" said the cat, but no one heard him.

Still, he didn't lose heart and played with a ball that he dropped down the stairs and then went after it. Playing and sleeping, sleeping and playing – and then suddenly it was evening again…

"Fred is so forgetful," thought the cat. "Who knows how long it will be before he realizes that I am sitting here alone, without food and drink? I have to think of something… Wait a minute… I have to get someone's attention somehow. How? Meowing really loud is no use, nobody will hear me. What can I do…"

Suddenly he knew.

The neighbours were back home. They loved piano music so much, didn't they? Fortunately, the lid of the piano was still open, so that his paws could touch the white and black keys.

The neighbours just had dinner and were now drinking coffee. Just as the neighbour was about to take a sip, he heard something in the house next door and said to his wife:

"Hush… I think Fred is back at his piano!"

"That would be great," said his wife, "because there aren't many people who can play as beautifully as Fred. I'm glad we can always listen to his music because the piano is right up against the wall."

But what they heard was definitely not a beautiful piano playing…

Oh, how false that sounded! The neighbours couldn't stand this and looked at each other in bewilderment.

"My poor ears hurt!" said the neighbour. "I'm going to see what's going on there. If Fred is playing false notes like that, he might be very sick…"

He grabbed the key and ran outside.

It was dark in Fred's house, but he still heard those false tones.

So he opened the door and turned on the light in the living room.

And there he saw… the cat! He ran back and forth as fast as he could over the keys of the piano, and now he meowed as well.

The neighbour immediately understood what was going on and exclaimed, holding his hands to his ears:

"Please stop, cat! I'll make sure you have enough food right away until Fred gets back. Please stop with that horrible music!"

It wasn't until the forgetful Fred came back that he remembered he'd forgotten to put water and food down for his cat. When he heard who took care of the cat, he bought a large bunch of flowers for his neighbours.

From now on he would make sure that he never left his cat alone for that long again.

And that was the end of the adventure, but everyone in the street knows what happened and all the people are so proud that one of the neighbours has a cat who plays the piano – even though his music sounds very out of tune…

21

WHAT KIND OF DOG IS THIS?

For Lisa, a great wish had come true. On her birthday she woke up very early and... immediately she knew what she was getting! Because downstairs, in the living room, came the high, shrill bark of a young dog! Never before had she brushed her teeth, washed and dressed so quickly. Once downstairs, she first met the dog she would soon come to love so much.

She called him Spot because he was stark white and only had a black spot under his right eye. It was a sweet and smart dog. He was happy with Lisa and followed her everywhere. When a dog show was being held in her hometown, she went there with Spot. A competition was held; who had the most beautiful dog? The big hall was very busy.

Many people also brought their own dogs and registered for the competition.

"This is Thor, a German Shepherd," she heard someone say as she stood in line to buy a ticket.

Someone else said, "I'm competing with my poodle."

There were terriers, greyhounds, boxers, wolfhounds, spaniels, collies...

"This is Spot," Lisa said proudly. "I would like a ticket and I also want Spot to register for the competition."

The ticket seller looked at her with raised eyebrows.

"What kind of breed is Spot?" he wanted to know.

Surprised, Lisa shrugged.

She had never thought about it that way.

"I don't know, sir."

"Well," said the man, "we call it a mongrel. A dog like yours can't compete. You can go in with Spot, but leave the competition to the purebred dogs."

Disappointed, she went in. Together with Spot, she walked past all those beautiful purebred dogs. A boy came up to her and handed her a card.

"For you," he said. "My name is Pim and my father organized this exhibition. We were at the cash register when we heard that Spot was not allowed to participate. Well, that's a mistake. All dogs count. Also the mongrels. And that Spot of yours is a very beautiful dog."

Lisa couldn't believe her ears. Pim took her to a corner of the large hall, where all the dogs were inspected. A group of men and women looked at Spot from head to toe. They even looked into his ears and into his faithful dog eyes. They stroked his head and watched him walk back and forth with Lisa.

"Hmm," they said; no more than that. Just: "Hmm..."

Pim's father appeared in the hall. He had a microphone with him and welcomed everyone. He said the result of the competition was announced.

"Number three is Thor the German Shepherd!" he cried. "A beautiful dog!"

There was cheering and loud applause.

"Second prize goes to Pop the Poodle, an amazing animal!"

The people cheered again and applauded again. Then it got quiet. Very quiet.

"First prize..." came the voice of Pim's father. "First prize goes to... Spot! Lisa, would you come forward with your amazing dog?"

Lisa had never been so proud. As the people clapped again, she climbed the stage and showed her faithful dog to everyone. She got a silver cup from Pim's father and Spot got a ribbon around his neck with a gold medal on it.

"What kind of dog is that anyway?" shouted someone from the audience.

Pim's father held the microphone in front of Lisa's mouth. She didn't have to think long about it.

Spontaneously she exclaimed:

"What is Stain for a dog...? Well, it is a True Friend Dog and there is only one of it in the whole world!"

Everyone laughed and Pim's father said: "So it's a unique dog too! There is only one dog like Spot and we can all see that Lisa is proud of him. Ladies and gentlemen, an extra loud round of applause for Lisa and for the True Friend Dog!"

Lisa bowed deeply. Spot wagged his tail and let out a cheerful bark.

When she walked through the hall with her dog again, she heard from all sides: "Congratulations! You have earned it because Spot the True Friend Dog is probably the sweetest dog there is."

Pim also came to congratulate her:

"I'm happy for you Lisa. And of course, I'm happy for Spot. Because he is a really nice dog."

Well, Lisa hadn't counted on that at all. She still has Spot and she loves him very much.

Spot may also be the only dog in the world who drinks water from… a silver cup every day!

THE EXHAUSTED ZOOKEEPER

22

When someone is exhausted, it means that he is too tired to stay on his feet. Such a person only thinks about sleeping, sleeping, sleeping...

Hear what happened to the keeper of the big zoo in the city. It was full summer. For days in a row, the temperature in the afternoon rose to more than thirty degrees, so that there was a real heat wave.

It was the task of keeper Jake to ensure that all animals had enough to drink. However, he did much more.

Water taps were installed throughout the zoo. Jake hooked up a garden hose and started watering the animals. The elephants especially loved it. As soon as they saw him coming, they ran to the front of their property and Jake shot the water jet over the fence. The animals trumpeted with delight and enjoyed the cold water splashing on their heated skin. Jake made sure the penguins had enough water and also filled the tigers' pond.

Yes, because tigers love getting into the water, especially when the weather is this warm. The cockatoos and parrots were cooled down when Jan used a large plant sprayer; they shook their feathers and spread their wings to catch as much of the tiny, fine droplets as possible. The zookeeper went on again. There were so many other animals that longed for water! Jake himself had gotten very tired by now...

He regularly wiped the sweat from his forehead:

"It's never been this hot," he sighed.

When he had visited all the animals, he could start again and so he ended up with the elephants for the second time that day. The tigers, the cockatoos, the parrots, all the animals saw the hard-working keeper again. After that, there was still more to do. Because of this beautiful weather, most of the animals were in their outdoor enclosure and now there was an opportunity to thoroughly clean the cages.

So Jake went from cage to cage and sprayed all the rubbish and started scrubbing hard. Every now and then he really needed to rest. He felt a little dizzy. Late in the afternoon, he came to the part of the zoo where the monkeys lived. All chimpanzees, orangutans, gorillas, baboons, mandrills and gibbons were outside.

They didn't play, no, they sat in the shade of the trees and kept calm in this sweltering heat.

Jake connected the garden hose and sprayed the floors of the monkey cages.

At last, he was in a large room where the chimpanzees lived.

There he also started to scrub and mop and then he really had to rest for a while. Caretaker Jake slumped to the cool floor, his back against a wall.

"I'm exhausted..." he whispered. "Oh, oh, how tired I am! I need some sleep, oh yes, I really need some sleep, some sleep..."

Soon he was snoring.

Visitors to the zoo couldn't believe their eyes as they walked past the chimpanzees' cage. They heard the loud snoring and then saw the keeper lying there. Among the visitors was a journalist from the city newspaper. He never went anywhere without his camera. And so he took a nice picture of the sleeping Jake.

When Jake arrived at work the next morning, he was met by the director. He showed him a photo that appeared in the morning paper.

Jake saw himself completely exhausted in the cage and read the caption: "Exhausted zookeeper sleeping in a chimpanzees' cage... No time for monkey business for the zookeeper... He was not going ape, no time to monkey around... All he needed was his rest..."

Jake became a little scared. Would he be scolded for falling asleep at work? But the director thought very differently about this: "As long as it has been this warm, you have been fully committed to the animals in our garden. You are our hero, Jake! You kept the animals cool and you cleaned all their cages. Today you'll have to do nothing at all! And you get extra money to buy a very, very big ice cream!"

Jake liked that, but he wondered who would take care of the animals today. Because it promised to be another hot day. The director rolled up his sleeves and said:

"Don't worry, Jake. Today I take care of everything!"

And so it happened that Jake sat in a cool ice cream parlour that day, enjoying a delicious ice cream.

And let's be honest - he really deserved that, didn't he?

23

CAT AND MOUSE

Every now and then animals that don't seem to fit together at all make friends.

There are stories of true friendship between a dog and a bear, a rabbit and a chicken, a turkey and a horse, a rat and a monkey, a cow and a crow and so on...

No one will easily believe that things can go very well between a cat and a mouse.

It's not for nothing that we could say about two people who are always arguing: "They act like cat and mouse."

Still, Oscar, the cat's best friend is none other than Marco the mouse! Oscar lived in a nice house and had a good life. But one day his owner moved. Of course, Oscar had to come along and when the moving van was at the door, he was picked up by strange hands and put in a tight cage. Of course, Oscar didn't feel like that at all and he lashed out with a sharp claw and jumped outside. The cat fled…

And so his boss went to his new home alone… hundreds of miles away. He came back a few more times to look for his cat, but Oscar was not to be found! It's also amazing that stories keep popping up about dogs and cats getting lost or left alone and then, over time, managing to return to their owners.

Oscar didn't like being all alone like that. Other people had come to live in his master's old house, and when he once appeared in the garden, he was chased away. It was time to find his owner.

Oscar went on a journey…

And that wasn't easy…

He had to cross busy streets, get across a river, go through dense forests, and even climb a high mountain. He was hungry and thirsty and his paws started to hurt. Still, Oscar persisted. He would sometimes find some food in a garbage can, or he would sneak into people's houses and look for something tasty in the kitchen. He drank rainwater from puddles or quenched his thirst with water from a stream or lake.

Cats are mysterious animals. How do they know the way? How do they find their owner? Perhaps that will always remain a mystery. Anyway, Oscar didn't give up. He slept in bushes and barns and as soon as it got light he got up and went on again. Yet one day this brave tomcat was at his wits' end. Despondent, he wondered if he would ever reach his goal. He trudged along on his sore legs.

He was about to cross the road near a small village when he saw a grey mouse sitting in the grass.

"I'm going to catch it!" he thought. "I'll get that one…"

He sat there silently looking at the mouse, and suddenly a completely different thought occurred to him:

"Oh, if I only found my master and had a warm house to sleep in again… I'd give anything for that. Yes, I would even befriend that mouse there if I could see my owner again!"

At that moment a door opened in a house on the outskirts of the village. Oscar looked in amazement at the man who walked into the garden there! Because that was, really, his own boss! He had found him! He was finally home!

"Mouse… mouse!" he said.

The grey mouse looked up and was startled.

"Fear not, good mouse. I'm Oscar the tomcat… from now on a real mouse friend! And what is your name?"

The mouse squeaked:

"Marco… Are you really a mouse friend?" "

"Yes I certainly am!" said Oscar. "Are you looking for a roof over your head, Marco? Do you want to eat well every day and sleep safely every night? Then come with me…"

The cat's owner was so happy! He finally had Oscar back! He cheered and hugged the weary tomcat.

Only much later did he find out that Oscar had not come home alone. Wherever he went, he was always in the company of a grey mouse.

That was a miracle!

It remained a mystery to his owner why such a large tomcat had befriended such a small mouse. But he really liked it and that's why he looked after Marco just as well as Oscar.

And so the cat and the mouse had a great life together!

24

A COAT FOR JACK FROST

The Black Forest was owned by Count Otto. He often went hunting there. None of his subjects was allowed to come there just like that. It was forbidden to gather wood for the fire. That is why people were often cold in winter. After all, the fireplace could not burn without wood.

"Please, Count," the people begged when the weather was bitterly cold. "Allow us to go into the Black Forest to chop wood."

The count's answer was always the same:

"Oh, it's not that cold, is it? You know what? When Jack Frost himself wears a coat to protect himself from the cold, you may all get wood from the Black Forest."

Jack Frost? He didn't exist, did he? Who had ever seen Jack Frost? Thus it was that the people shivered again with cold when winter came. In the house, they wore thick coats and slept under a thick pile of blankets. It was freezing, it was storming, it was snowing. The world was white. Even the Black Forest was white... Someone knocked on the gate of the castle.

"Count Otto! We are so cold! We need wood!"

The Count, sitting by the warm hearth, rose, opened a window, and cried:

"Go away! Only when Jack Frost himself wears a coat, everyone will be allowed to go to the forest and cut wood!"

The window closed with a bang.

It got colder and colder, there was a sharp frost!

Emperor Charlemagne passed through the country. He was on his way to an important meeting. He rode in a large carriage drawn by eight big horses. He stopped the carriage at the Black Forest. A large tent was set up for him and his soldiers cut wood in the forest and built great fires. Emperor Charlemagne and his soldiers were not cold! After a hot meal, they made a big snowman together. Everyone laughed when the emperor went to get a coat and put it around the snowman's shoulders. He even put a golden crown on the white, round head of the snowman and said:

"I crown you king. You are... King Winter, you are the one and only mighty Jack Frost!"

Then he retired to his tent and went to sleep. The next morning the snowman was still there. The king woke up because he heard a noise. He heard voices. People were singing! He quickly dressed and came out of his tent. A hundred people danced in a circle around the crowned snowman. His soldiers were smiling.

"Emperor! Look! The people are singing and dancing and it seems they are not cold at all!"

The emperor didn't understand.

"Have one of these people come to me and explain," he said.

A little later he spoke to a man who told him everything about Count Otto.

The emperor didn't have to think long about what to do next. He immediately sent soldiers to the castle to collect the count in the big carriage.

When he arrived, people were still dancing around the crowned snowman.

The Count bowed to the Emperor.

But the Emperor spoke in a loud voice for all to hear:

"No, no, don't bow to me, bow to Jack Frost and keep your promise!"

Of course, Count Otto could not refuse an order from his Emperor. People saw with their own eyes how he walked through the snow and bowed deeply to the snowman.

"Jack Frost," said the Earl, "I see you are wearing a coat. That is why people are now allowed to go into the Black Forest to chop wood."

Everyone started cheering. Again the people danced around the snowman.

And... the Emperor's soldiers, Count Otto and even Emperor Charlemagne all danced along! Then the people went with axes and saw into the forest. They gathered wood and cut down trees.

That evening it was warm in all the houses.

Emperor Charlemagne continued with his carriage.

The snowman no longer wore a crown. But... he was still wearing the jacket!

The emperor had not taken it from him..!

25

This is the wonderful story of Victor Finch, a small bird from the Low Countries. He was smart, always friendly and cheerful, and all the other birds liked him. He just didn't like winter. When it got cold and even a large number of starlings flew to the south of England to hibernate there, Victor Finch would sit shivering on a branch.

Other finches, sparrows, crows, thrushes and magpies did not understand him:

"Why are you shivering there, Victor! A little cold isn't bad at all, is it?"

"Brr!" Victor would say. "A little cold? I'm almost freezing! Give me the summer with the warm sun!"

He had heard great tales of the journeys of large birds with long legs, huge wings, and red beaks. Storks...! However, he had never seen a stork. A crow had once told him that storks flew to distant, warm Africa every winter.

Only when spring came again in the low countries they did return.

"That's nice," said Victor. "I would like to do that too. But I'm too small and my wings can't carry me that far. I don't even know which direction I'd have to fly to get to Africa!"

It was getting colder again and Victor had been shivering on a branch one night. In the morning he awoke to an unfamiliar voice. On a higher branch sat... a giant bird with long legs and a red bill.

"Hello," said the strange bird. "Are you Victor Finch?"

"Um, yes..." the little bird replied. "You look like a... like a stork!"

The big bird laughed and shook its feathers.

"You're right. I am a stork. Now I heard from the birds here that you hate winter. Tomorrow I leave with a few storks to warm Africa. Would you like to join us? Then you can finally go on holiday."

Victor shook his little head.

"How nice of you to offer that. But I can't possibly keep up with you. You have those big wings… No, Africa is too far for me."

"No problem," said the stork. "You just sit on my back. You don't weigh much. After a while, you can sit on the back of another stork. This is how we'll all bring you to the warmth and that's how we'll bring you back again. I have heard from everyone that you are such a nice bird and that is why we would love to help you!"

Victor could hardly believe it. And yet it was true! The next morning a dozen storks alighted on the branches. Victor flew to the stork he had met the other day and jumped on his back.

"Here we go!" laughed the stork. "See you all, we'll be back in the spring!"

The twelve storks flew away and they were waved off by all the birds that stayed at home – the sparrows, starlings, crows, finches and magpies.

"Victor goes to Africa!" sighed a starling. "That is a lot further than the south of England. Trust me… that is very, very far away!"

The birds eagerly looked forward to spring.

And when the weather finally became nice and warm again, the twelve storks returned.

High in the air, Victor Finch jumped from the back of a stork and flew under his own power to the branch he always liked to sit on.

Moments later, hundreds of birds perched on the branches of that same tree.

Yet it was very quiet. Because everyone wanted to be able to hear the little finch's voice when he started talking about his fantastic holiday in far-off Africa.

Because Victor is the only finch from the Low Countries that has actually been there!

Thanks to the help of twelve friendly storks...

26

Old Bert had worked on his farm all his life. He had never been on vacation. Year after year he had worked the land and looked after the animals. Now his son would take over the farm. Farmer Bert was offered a trip by family, friends and acquaintances.

"You are going by plane to a tropical island," he was told.

Frankly, the farmer would have preferred to stay at home, but he didn't want to refuse the gift, so he had himself taken to the airport. He was carrying a suitcase of clothes and... a big black umbrella!

"Leave it at home!" said everyone, "you don't need it there. The weather is always nice on that island."

But farmer Bert and his umbrella were inseparable and so he took it with him! When he arrived on the island, he was amazed. White beaches, a blue sea, palm trees everywhere...

He had never seen anything like it.

The people of the island had to laugh a bit when they saw farmer Bert...

"He is the first tourist to bring an umbrella," they said. "Look! Even when he's walking on the beach, he keeps that silly umbrella under his arm."

He soon had a nickname: Bert Umbrella!

It was full summer. Every day it got warmer on the island. Yes, it was sweltering! The residents soon agreed that it had never been this hot before. Even the oldest residents could not remember that the temperature had risen so high.

"This is unbearable!" the people puffed. "We are really used to something, but this is crazy."

They stayed indoors as much as possible. But then again, there was shopping to be done, there was work to be done... Sooner or later everyone had to go outside anyway. And that was no fun! The sun, that great glowing fireball, was high in the blue sky and its bright rays scorched the island!

Farmer Bert walked through the streets. He had unfolded his good old umbrella and held it over his head. In this way, he protected himself from the bright rays of the sun. Yes, he was warm, of course, but he wasn't as bothered by the heat as the islanders. Farmer Bert noticed that and they stared after him in amazement.

"Look at this! That weird tourist! It rarely rains on our island, so none of us owns an umbrella. Now, look what farmer Bas uses his umbrella for! How smart! How handy! This is amazing! He has found a way to be able to walk outside and still stay out of the sun."

The next day a plane landed with a large order; an umbrella for every islander! Soon no one was out on the street without an umbrella. Farmer Bert was offered an extensive meal in the most expensive restaurant on the island and he received the most beautiful gifts. Everyone thanked him for his idea of using an umbrella in the summer.

Farmer Bert was happy with all that compliments, but he was even more happy when he was back home on the big farm. His family, friends and acquaintances came to see him and asked if he had had a good time.

"It was nice to be on that island," he said. "It was beautiful there. It was also very hot. And it never rained. That's why I was glad I had my umbrella with me."

Nobody understood that. Could farmer Bert have suffered sunstroke and was that the reason why he said such nonsensical things?

Yes, everyone really thought that the long journey had confused him a little when the farmer laughed and spoke in a loud voice:

"Do you know who I am? I am none other than... Bert Umbrella!"

And the tropical island... Believe it or not, it's called Umbrella Island these days!

27

ICE CUBES FOR THE SULTAN

The most beautiful building in the country was the sultan's palace! The floors were made of the most expensive marble, the roofs of pure gold. It must have been great to work there. But it was said that the sultan didn't just hire just anyone.

He wanted only the very best cooks, chamberlains, and servants. Everyone who came to apply was subjected to a thorough test.

The sultan's imagination knew no bounds!

A young man by the name of Bobo, for example, wanted to be a servant in the palace. The sultan received him in the garden.

"Do you think you'll be a good servant, young man?" he asked.

"Oh yes, great Sultan," replied Bobo, bowing deeply. "I can work hard and no effort is too much for me."

The sultan smiled.

"We'll see," he said. "I'll give you an order."

He held up a glass filled with lemonade.

"Tomorrow I want an ice cube in my glass," he said, "because I like to drink my lemonade cold. Will you take care of that?"

Bobo bowed again.

"Certainly, great Sultan! I'm already on my way!"

It was never winter in the land of the sultan. It was always hot there. Bobo rented a camel and set out on a long, long journey. The camel grew tired and he exchanged it for another. It went on, right through the great land of the sultan. Again he changed camels and again and again...

At last, he came into the cold mountains and climbed up until he reached a peak where there was a thick layer of snow and where chilly caves were filled with ice.

He immediately went to work.

With an axe, he chopped off a huge chunk of ice. It was thirty feet high and thirty feet wide. With the help of mountain people, he managed to slide the large block down. There the log was lifted onto a wooden chariot pulled by twenty camels.

"Run, camels! run!" cried Bobo.

The animals did their utmost, but the cart started slowly. Soon Bobo had to change the animals again. It got warmer again. It was full summer in the empire of the sultan. The ice started to melt. Water dripped from the cart. The block got smaller and smaller. Fortunately, it also became lighter, so the camels had to pull less weight and could walk faster.

The block could be put on a smaller cart, and now it only took six camels to pull it. Would Bobo make it? Would there be any of the ice left when he finally reached the sultan's palace?

"Faster! Faster!" he kept calling.

Finally, no longer needing a cart, he rode a camel again, holding the ice in his hand…

"Faster! Oh, faster!"

The sultan was sitting in his garden and in front of him, on a small table, was a glass of lemonade. All his councillors sat around him; there were fifty of them! And everyone waited in silence for Bobo to appear. Finally, Bobo came into the garden! He was very tired, but he ran as fast as he could. Oh, what an effort he had taken to fulfil the sultan's wish! He could barely stand when he bowed deeply to the sultan and dropped a small ice cube into the glass of lemonade.

"Please, great Sultan, I hope you like it."

The councillors clapped their hands in admiration. The sultan picked up the glass and took a sip. Then he looked at Bobo and said:

"Excellent job, young man, excellent! You're exactly the servant I'm looking for. Come back tomorrow... with fifty ice cubes! Because all my councillors want to enjoy this too!"

Bobo's eyes widened.

He bowed, turned, left the palace garden and... never did the demanding sultan see him again...

That summer the circus had come again. Outside the village, the wagons were parked in a large field. Clowns walked back and forth in shoes that were too big, big predators growled in their cages.

Later the big tent would be set up.

But first, there would be a performance in the open air. The weather was so nice that the director of the circus decided to organize a free show on the field. The children of the village were curious and naturally went to take a look.

A very special number had been announced: a princess would just disappear into thin air. Wouldn't that be impossible? How could that be done? Even the mayor of the village came to take a look.

"I want to see this with my very own eyes!" he said. "Someone who vanishes into thin air just like that..."

When everyone was sitting on the grass, the circus director got out of his big trailer and welcomed the audience.

"Welcome, welcome on this beautiful summer day! The circus will show you all the animals and the clowns will make you laugh. And then, to top it all off, Princess Ara will show her disappearing act."

Now a colourful procession of horses, lions, tigers and elephants passed by. The clowns appeared. They tumbled through the grass, making jokes and juggling colourful balls. Everyone enjoyed. It was lovely to sit here and watch all the circus had to offer.

And then the princess appeared! Macaw was a little girl who wore a long red cloak and a crown of gold. She stood on the back of a white pony and seemed to have no trouble keeping her balance.

The pony stopped in the middle of the field.

A large number of children dressed as fairies danced near. They took each other by the hand, formed a circle around the pony, and jumped to the left en to the right. Two clowns carried a huge flag across the field.

"Please, pay attention, pay attention!" came the loud voice of the ringmaster. "Just wait a little while and then… the princess will be gone!"

The children watched intently and shouted:

"That's impossible, that isn't possible!"

The clowns held up the huge flag and the princess, the pony and the dancing elves disappeared from view for just a moment.

As they lowered the flag, the audience heaved a loud sigh of surprise…

There was the pony again! And there were the dancing elves holding each other by the hand. But Princess Ara was gone! She had become invisible as if she had disappeared into a hole in the ground!

How could that be?

The children stood up and clapped their hands enthusiastically.

The flag was raised again. When the clowns lowered it a second time, Princess Ara stood on the pony's back again and received deafening applause with a deep bow. Even the mayor applauded and cheered. Could Princess Ara really just disappear when she wanted to?

The children of the village would never know.

Only Amanda, the mayor's daughter, learned the secret. The little princess came to visit her and then she explained…

"It's very simple, Amanda," said Princess Ada. "Nobody counts the elves… The clowns are holding up the flag. I quickly take off my crown and take off the cloak. I hide it under the pony's saddle. I now have wings on my back and am dressed just like the other elves. There are eleven dancing elves. I am the twelfth. No one can tell the difference between eleven elves and twelve elves. The flag goes down and I'm not there anymore… Then the flag goes up again, I put on the cloak, put the crown on my head and jump on the back of the ferry and there I am again! Will you never betray my secret?"

That's what the mayor's daughter promised.

Won't you tell the princess's secret either…?

29

THE CHICKENS AND THE RABBIT

The six chickens on the large farm had a spacious coop and a beautiful run. This run, a walkway delimited by a high wire netting fence, was their abode for the day; at night they slept in the coop.

"If only we could take a look at the other side of the wire netting fence!" the chickens often clucked at each other. "How fantastic that would be. Then we went out into the wide world! Oh, a long walk across the yard, through the fields, to the woods in the distance…!"

Then all six of them stared through the mesh for a while and let out deep sighs.

It would always remain a dream.

Their world consisted of the coop and the run.

They would never get a chance to get out of there.

They saw the cows and the horses in the pasture. The dog in the yard. The pigeons happily flew back and forth.

It was such a beautiful, wonderfully warm summer; long days that were ideal for getting out and about. But the chickens had nowhere to go. Their wish would never come true.

One afternoon an animal appeared that they had never seen before. It had long ears and brown fur. It came along the run in small leaps.

"Who are you?" cackled a chicken.

"I am a rabbit," replied the animal. "Not a tame rabbit, but a wild rabbit! I can go where I want, I can do what I want!"

The chickens clucked in admiration.

"If only we were as free as you, rabbit! If only we could also do what we wanted, just like you!"

The rabbit looked surprised through the wire netting fence.

"What do you want then?"

The chickens clucked in unison:

"Outwards! Take a walk to the edge of the forest! Without the farmer seeing it, of course, because otherwise, he will immediately chase us back."

The rabbit thought for a moment and then said:

"I will help you. Tonight, when it starts to get dark, I'll be back!"

He kept his word. The chickens were already waiting for him by the wire netting fence. They watched in amazement as the rabbit began to dig a hole. A very big hole! He dug into the earth with his front legs, he kicked the earth away with his hind legs! He made a tunnel and ended up in the run with the chickens.

"Come on," he whispered. "Outwards! Everything is safe!"

The chickens could hardly believe it! One by one they crawled through the tunnel and then they stood on the other side of the run. They were free. And it was such a lovely, sultry summer evening! The rabbit skipped away and they followed him. Now the chickens did not cluck, they kept their beaks closed. They walked across the yard, passed through the meadow, and reached the edge of the forest.

When the rabbit skipped through the trees, they went after him again, and so they came for the first time in their lives into the great, cool forest. It was lovely. Now they were far enough from the farm to open their beaks again and they were cackling with delight.

"Thank you, dear rabbit! Thank you so much! How wonderful it is to be able to walk around so freely."

The rabbit saw that the chickens were really enjoying themselves. He decided to befriend them.

"When you're back in the run, we'll close the tunnel properly," he said. "Then the farmer will not see that you have been away. And as long as the weather stays nice, I'll come to you every evening at dusk and dig the tunnel again!"

He kept his word again. The summer was long and in the evening the rabbit appeared to free the chickens. They walked through the meadows and through the forest and felt happy.

Then it was autumn, with a lot of rain.

It was winter with lots of snow.

Then, on a warm, sunny spring day, the rabbit reappeared on the other side of the run.

"Hello, chickens!" he whispered. "Are you coming along?"

He started to dig a tunnel.

"Rabbit," whispered the chickens, "you are the sweetest animal in the whole world!"

And they slipped out one by one. Towards freedom...

"Come on," said the rabbit, as he began to skip. "I'll be back tomorrow and the day after tomorrow. I come to set you free every night as long as spring and summer last!"

Thanks to their special friendship with the rabbit, the six chickens got to know freedom and went on the most beautiful walks together...

30

THE BIGGEST LIE

It was a long, hot summer. King Rollo was bored. It was far too hot to go outside, and he sat all day on his throne in a cool room of his palace.

"I want to laugh, I want to have fun," he grumbled to his court jester. "I can dream of your silly jokes! Come up with something fun!"

The bright court jester immediately had an idea.

"Sire," he said, "let your subjects come to you. Everyone has to tell a lie. Whoever tells the biggest lie may dine with you and will receive a golden cup as a gift!"

CHILDREN'S SHORT STORIES

The king thought that was a good plan. The people were informed of the king's wish. But who dared come to the palace to tell the king a lie? On the other hand, it was a great honour to eat with the king and that golden cup must have been worth a fortune!

The first to try was a wealthy businessman.

He stood before the throne, bowed and said:

"Sire, I've lost all my money, I'm as poor as a church mouse!"

The king smiled.

"Nice lie," he said, "because you're almost as rich as I am!"

The second was a beggar clad in rags and said it the other way around:

"Sire, I am your richest subject, I swim in the money!"

The king laughed a little louder, but he didn't think this was worth a golden cup.

A woman appeared before the throne. Her face was bright red because it was so hot outside.

But she started to shiver and said:

"Do you know that it is twenty degrees below zero outside?"

King Rollo thought this was quite funny, although it didn't make him roar with laughter.

More and more people now came to the palace. They stood in a long line in the sunlit yard.

Once inside, the lies were told:

"I've been on the moon, I've lived there for twenty years..."

"I dug a tunnel and crawled into it. Suddenly I reappeared on the other side of the globe!"

The king no longer thought about the heat and was no longer bored. What a fantasy people had! They made up all sorts of things, hoping to get that golden cup.

"It's so hot that all the water in the river has evaporated. Now there are a hundred crocodiles in my pool. I just jump in when I want to swim."

"I can jump high, very high... If I want to get into my house, I just jump through the window. Oh yes, I live on the twentieth floor."

The king could not make a decision. There were a lot of big liars who were eligible for the dinner and the golden cup. But who would he award those prizes?

King Rollo couldn't figure it out.

His court jester said:

"Sire, there's someone else who wants to tell a lie. There's a little boy in the hallway."

The door swung open.

A funny little fellow went straight to the king and said in an angry voice:

"Go away! Go away, you hear? Outwards! Let me sit on the throne."

The king roared with laughter.

"Why would I do that?"

"Because I am the king!" cried the boy. "The throne is mine. And the crown too! Give it to me too, for I am the king of the land!"

King Rollo thought this was the biggest, but also the nicest lie.

The boy was allowed to sit on his throne and the king himself put his crown on his head.

Later the king ate with him and then he gave him the golden cup.

"You deserve it!"

The little fellow thanked, bowed, and then said:

CHILDREN'S SHORT STORIES

"Yet I am a true king... You have just made sure, Sire, that I am the king of liars!"

The boy held the expensive golden cup tightly in both hands and tripped out of the room with a proud face...

The king roared with laughter and his court jester laughed with him!

"I have never seen such a bright boy," said the king.

And that wasn't a lie...

31

CASPER AND HIS DOG

Casper had been given an important assignment. He had to bring a letter to the emperor. It was the middle of summer, the blazing sun was high in the sky and the road was long!

Casper had brought his faithful dog Max with him. The dog also suffered in the heat. He was panting heavily and walking more and more slowly.

"Come on now, Max!" said Casper repeatedly. "We have to move on! Don't give up!"

But Max was very tired. At the end of a village stood a large house. A man came out of the stable, followed by a donkey. He looked surprised at the dog.

"What a beautiful animal! I've always wanted to have a dog. Leave him here, young man, and you will have my donkey."

Casper looked at his tired, panting dog.

He himself was also exhausted and he understood that he could rest on the donkey's back.

And so he left his faithful dog and continued on the donkey...

He immediately regretted it deeply, but there was no turning back; the letter had to be delivered to the emperor as soon as possible!

He kept thinking about Max.

The next day it was even hotter.

The donkey began to walk more slowly. Casper came to a market and a merchant called to him:

"I see you have a nice donkey! Soon there will be someone who really wants to buy a donkey. Come on, trade him for this horse! Then we're both in luck - I'll sell the donkey for a lot of money and you'll have a rested horse to continue your journey on."

And so, a moment later, Casper rode a horse through the sun-drenched land.

At night he slept in an inn.

In the morning, when he was about to go on again, a man approached him.

"I see you have a beautiful horse. I need a horse to pull a cart. Do you want to exchange the horse for a large camel? A camel can withstand the heat better than a horse."

Casper agreed and so it happened that he continued his journey on a camel. And his thoughts were still with the dog he'd left behind. One afternoon he passed a site where a circus tent was being set up.

"A camel! A camel!" cried the boss of the circus, when he saw Casper approaching. "How I would love to have a camel for my circus. I have a good idea, young man. Give me the camel, and I'll give you one of my elephants!"

Casper was interested in this. Moments later, he owned a large, strong elephant that took him straight to the emperor's palace. There he delivered the letter and he slept in a tower room. The elephant was allowed to stand in a large stable with the imperial horses. Casper slept badly. He dreamed of Max. Oh, how he regretted leaving his dog behind!

Early in the morning, he left the palace. The strong elephant didn't seem bothered by the heat at all and walked on briskly. He passed the circus. There the boss was still very happy with the camel. He never saw the horse and donkey again.

Then, after a long journey, he passed the house again where he had traded Max for the donkey.

Max was in the garden. As soon as he saw Casper coming, he sprang to his feet and ran towards him. Casper jumped off the elephant's high back and knelt to hug his dog.

"Max! How I have missed you!"

Max was happy! The dog wagged his tail and barked.

"An elephant! What a beautiful animal!" Casper heard someone say.

He looked up and saw the man who had traded Max for the donkey.

"Can we make a deal?" asked Casper. "You get the elephant and I get my dog back."

"An excellent idea!" said the man. "That elephant is worth a fortune. Come in, young man, and you will be given food and drink. Here you can rest. Don't go back until tomorrow..."

Casper thought that was a good idea. That night he slept soundly, with his faithful dog watching over him.

In the morning he went home with Max and left the elephant behind. As he walked he repeatedly stroked the large head of the dog and then said with a sigh:

"Max, you are my best friend. I'll never let you down again! Never again! I solemnly promise you that!"

Max wagged his tail and barked happily.

Casper and his dog Max... they are real friends, you always see them together.

32

It had been sweltering hot in the vast African savannah for several months. The grass had withered. The few trees offered little shade.

At night it cooled down for a while, but early in the morning, it was already so hot that the animals could hardly stand it anymore. All the beasts roamed the land in search of water. However, the river had dried up completely.

Only here and there was a pool left in which the fish had gathered. The elephants fanned themselves with their large ears. The zebras trudged past the lazy lions dozing with closed eyes. Animals of all kinds roamed the dry river bed, searching for water.

"I'm very old," muttered a huge, wrinkled elephant, "but I don't remember it ever being this hot. And so long in a row…"

Somewhere, in the middle of the river, a pool had been left behind. There was still quite a bit of water in it. At first, the pool was inhabited only by fish and crocodiles. Then a group of hippos arrived. They all dived into the pool.

"Hello there… can't you just be a little careful with those fat, cumbersome bodies?" grumbled the crocodiles.

"Don't worry," said a hippo. "There is room enough for all of us."

In the evening giraffes, gnus and zebras came to drink from the pool. The crocodiles didn't like that either.

"Don't drink so much!" they cried. "Soon the pool will be completely empty!"

"We are thirsty," was the reply. "There is enough water for everyone."

The old elephant led the herd through the riverbed and reached the pool one afternoon when the sun was at its highest point in the sky. Relieved, he began to trumpet loudly.

"Water, friends! Water! Here we can drink, here we can roll in the mud!"

"Don't! Don't, you hear?" exclaimed a crocodile, startled. "You will crush us under your enormous weight!"

However, the elephants didn't care. They all drank as much as they could and then walked into the water. Even the fat hippos had to move aside. Now it started to get very full in the pool! But the elephants didn't go away.

"Everybody move a bit!" cried the great elephant. "Come on, friends, make some room!"

That day more animals came to the pool. Huge snakes slid into the water, birds descended from the cloudless sky, more deer, more giraffes and more gnus appeared, followed by a large herd of zebras. Then the pool was full. Packed full!

There was no more room for other visitors!

Hyenas, leopards and lions came to drink.

It became night. Finally, it cooled down a bit. Some animals crawled out of the pool.

But the next morning, when it had quickly become sweltering again, everyone quickly went back to the water.

More elephants appeared, a hippopotamus, a few lizards and more than fifty antelopes.

"Move up!" cried the old elephant, just like the day before. "Move up!"

But most of the animals had to stay aside. The crocodiles no longer grumbled. They understood that it was useless. Everyone needed water. The animals had to share the water with each other...

Then a large bird of prey flew over the pool.

"Hello down there!" he croaked, "may I have your attention? You can't see much from the pool, you face the side of the dried-up river. Good news, animals! Dark clouds are coming... It's going to rain!"

Everyone cheered. The bird of prey was right. The clouds were already floating over the pool. The rain pattered down. That night the river again filled with water and the pool was absorbed into it. The animals said goodbye to each other:

"Bye! Maybe we'll see each other again next year... in the last pool left by then."

Especially the crocodiles sighed deeply:

"Finally we have space again. Because it's hard to get stuck between a giant elephant and a fat hippo!"

33

L ittle Monika was deep under the covers in her bed. It was the middle of winter and it was freezing outside. Rarely had it been this cold. There were frost flowers on the windows.

Monika was almost asleep when she suddenly heard something. There was a tap on the window. Immediately he was wide awake. She listened. The tapping sounded again. She got out of her warm bed and went to the window. She opened the curtain. It was a clear night. The moon was full. The light shone through the thick ice flowers. She carefully opened the window. Now the moonlight was shining brightly inside. Something fell on the windowsill. Little Monika's mouth fell open when she saw what it was.

　　　　　　　　　　　　　　CHILDREN'S SHORT STORIES

An elf! A slender, trembling figure with a white face and flapping wings. Very softly she heard the elf say:

"Cold! Cold! We're freezing! Help us!"

Just then, more elves landed on the windowsill. Monika counted ten of them! She quickly closed the window and turned on the light in her room. Carefully she picked up the trembling elves and held them in her arms. That way she could warm them. Sitting on the edge of her bed, she looked at the little figures. The elves got some colour in their faces again. The same small voice from before was heard again:

"Thank you, girl, thank you so much. You saved us all. What's your name?"

"Monika..." she said.

"What a beautiful name," said the elf. "You know... Elves never really show themselves to people. But one of us pronounced a wrong spell and suddenly we flew through the dark night and it became freezing cold. We got so cold that we couldn't think clearly. None of us could cast another spell that would bring us back to the land of elves and gnomes."

Monika nodded. "I believe I understand," she said. "How exciting that I can really see you now. Are you getting warmer yet?"

"Yes," the elf sighed. "Fortunately. My magic is coming back. If you hadn't saved us, if you hadn't opened your window for us, if you hadn't taken us in your arms... Then things would have gone wrong for us. Thank you, Monika! Thank you!"

The other elves looked up at her and repeated the words:

"Thank you, Monika! Thank you!"

Then she was asked to open the window again. The elves flew to the windowsill. Their wings moved very quickly. They all started to mumble. It sounded like the chirping of birds.

"The magic spell!" thought Monika.

The elves descended, waved at her, and then disappeared through the open window into the cold night.

"Goodbye elves!" said Monika.

She looked outside. The elves flew through the moonlit night and then suddenly there was a blinding light, like ten stars bursting apart. The elves were gone. Monika closed the window, turned off the light and crawled into bed shivering.

"They're back in the land of elves and gnomes," she thought and fell asleep with a smile on her lips.

When she awoke the next morning, she went to the window and opened it.

It was now light outside. It had snowed. Monika thought of the elves and shook her head.

"It can't be true," she sighed. "I must have dreamed it all..."

Or not? Had it been a dream or had she really seen elves? She would never know.

Dream or reality, she kept a very nice memory of it...

Because every day she thinks of the little elves who were so cold that they forgot their magic spells!

34

A GOOD IDEA FROM A LITTLE SQUIRREL

All the older squirrels told the same story to the young squirrels: "In spring, summer and autumn you can find food everywhere. In winter there is virtually nothing. Make sure to stock up. Hide tasty snacks, remember those spots well! Then you can easily get through the winter. When you are hungry, you go to such a place and take out the food again."

The little squirrels had listened carefully. They went in search of food, ate as much as they could and didn't forget to hide something everywhere. Winter came. Food became scarce. Now it was time for the little squirrels to gather their supplies. They knew exactly where they had hidden everything: under the roots of an old oak tree, in a hollow chestnut tree, in an abandoned fox den...

Still, the little squirrels hadn't everything under control. It had started snowing. Everywhere was a pack of snow almost two feet thick…

Where was the old oak, where was the chestnut tree, where was the abandoned den? They climbed into the branches of the trees and looked down.

Everything was white beneath them.

Now the winter lasted a very long time!

The squirrels were very hungry.

Finally, finally it was spring again.

"We have to do it differently," little Wooltail said to his friends. "Otherwise we will be so hungry again next winter."

"Then what should we do?" his friends wanted to know.

Wooltail explained.

"We have to work together, we have to share everything. Ask other animals if we can stock up at their homes. Even if there is still such a thick layer of snow, we always know where the owl lives, where the rabbits live, where the woodpecker has his house..."

"Good idea!" his friends exclaimed, "that's going to be a lot of fun!"

Wooltail himself went to Bob the tawny owl, who agreed that he should stock up on nuts in his spacious home in a hollow lime tree.

It was winter again. There was even more snow than last year! Everything was white. But now the squirrels no longer had to search for their supplies. Everyone was hungry and they met for the first time in the tawny owl's house. There the squirrels sat together, enjoying the nuts the clever Wooltail had kept there.

"Tomorrow they will all go to Rod the Rabbit," said a squirrel. "I packed a cupboard full of walnuts, beechnuts and hazelnuts."

The owl had to laugh.

"You owe this all to a little squirrel that's even smarter than a wise owl," he said. "Wooltail's idea saved you all!"

The squirrels agreed.

"Yes, he has ensured that we can continue to eat our fill in the winter. We will do it this way every year from now on. Then in the winter we can always sit together and enjoy extensive meals."

The squirrels met the next evening at Rod the Rabbit, the next day they were the guest of a woodpecker and then they went to visit a badger. Winter flew by before they knew it, spring was just around the corner.

When older squirrels asked; "How did you get through the winter?" the little squirrels slapped their over-eaten bellies and said with a laugh; "Good, very good! Thanks to the clever idea of little Wooltail...!"

THE BIGGEST SNOWMAN

35

The children of the village cheered! Last night there was a huge amount of snow. That meant that the big game of the winter was to be held again; who made the biggest, the tallest snowman? There were great prizes waiting for the winner. A silver cup and a new wooden sledge! Last year a group of children made a snowman that was almost 12 feet high.

"This year we are making a higher one!" the children said.

It was still early in the morning when everyone gathered in a large field outside the village. There was more than enough snow to make giant snowmen. Soon the children split into two groups.

"We are going to win!" spoke the first group. "Just like last year! The cup and the sledge are ours!"

The children from the other group laughed and said:

"Just wait and see. Our snowman is going to be a little taller than yours!"

The mayor was also present and he gave the go-ahead:

"Go on! Let's see what you can do! We want to see huge snowmen!"

The children got to work. Together they began to roll large snowballs across the field. They got bigger and bigger.

Everyone participated.

Except for Little John.

"You're in the way, Little Johnny!" said the children from the first group. "You'd better go home, you're much too small!"

"You can't join us," said the children from the second group. "We can miss a little guy like you like a toothache."

Little Johnny shrugged.

"Then I'll make my own snowman," he said and began to roll a snowball across the field. His doll was soon ready. He was less than three feet high, as small as Little Johnny himself...

The children piled the big snowballs on top of each other. They even needed ladders and with combined forces, they managed to lift the heaviest snowballs. Last year's record was easily broken. The dolls were already higher than twelve! thirteen feet... thirteen and a half feet... fourteen feet!

These weren't ordinary snowmen anymore, these were snow giants! And they were exactly the same height. Two boys climbed the long ladders.

The first had brought a top hat, which he wanted to put on the snowman's head:

"Then we have the tallest doll!"

The other boy was also carrying a top hat.

"Our snowman will be the tallest!"

Now both giant dolls wore hats. The ladders were removed. The mayor came to see which doll was the tallest.

And then... then a storm arose. The giant dolls moved back and forth. They fell towards each other. The top hats were already falling to the ground. Then the dolls clapped together and the snowballs rolled down and shattered. What a disappointment!

"The dolls were so big they had to fall," the mayor said. "They were just top-heavy! The fierce wind threw them off balance. Now no one has won!"

But... was that true? Was there no winner this year?

"Mayor! Look at Little John's snowman!" someone shouted. "It's only a small snowman, but because it's the only one, it's also the biggest! Little John has won the competition of the year!"

The mayor laughed and nodded enthusiastically:

"Yes, Little John is the winner!"

A little later Johnny was pulled through the village on his brand-new sleigh and he held up the silver cup with pride.

He wasn't allowed to join one of the two groups... and then he won the top prize all by himself...